NIGHT WAVE

A Novel By *Todd La Croix*

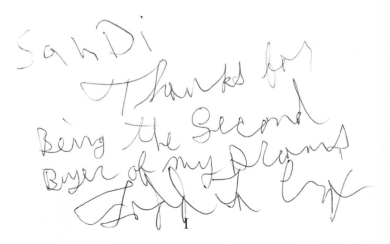

SahDi

Thanks for
Being the Second
Buyer of my Dreams

1

Todd La Croix

Amazon CreateSpace Publishing
www.createspace.com

The Author's Websites

http://amazon.com/author/toddlacroix

http://delphius.weebly.com

ISBN 978-1483910154

ISBN 1483910156

ASIN BOOBXT2B7M

S*pecial Thanks*

Goes out to the many people who helped nourish my creative nature through the years; I know it has not always been easy. Many thanks goes to Connie, Chris and Varonica, Royce Hobbs, Eva, Bamboo, T, Julie, Shadow, Ian and Emily, Brandon, Dave and the whole *'Dali High'* Crew; along with the *Infamous* Mr. Burns in Dali China; it was always a lively conversation to say the least. They are the ones who gave me back something I had almost lost, HOPE.

Also, a big thanks goes to: Doug Smith for the Editing, Sharon and Dennis McCarthy, Oscar Xavier Del Sebastian, Thomas Corr, Bee Vang and John D. Alexander; who helped to make this novel exist through their belief in my talent. Chris Kinghall, Brian Johns, Alex Hirka, Michael Nedell, Mark Pekar, Ishmael and Grace Ahmed, Mathew Brand, Kenny and Charlie, Rob Carstairs, Devon Ewalt, Andy Lugo, Scotty and Transplante. And the whole "Java-Love" Community.

Tim Elliot and Avery Rifken for being the best bosses to ever fire me, *repeatedly,* and for making the best soul food a starving artist had on a consistent basis. Mark Mckinnon, and David Francis for being the best teachers a broken kid like me could have. I can philosophize and cook at the same time because of the two of you. Respect.

A shout out to the *Bad Monkey* posse, and they who returned to me something I could not have lived without; my passport and camera. Keep on *Rocking* in the PRC.

A mention and appreciation goes to a man named Neyma, who once helped me out at a low moment in Thailand, when most might have not, and who showed me the power of the I-Ching.

I even must begrudgingly thank my Ex-wife, for gracing herself as the mother of my awesome children; as well as the cover of this novel.

Especially big thanks goes to Angela Gale for giving me her inspiring friendship through the years, and for drawing me the **Delphius Dragon** so many years ago.

Thank you all for believing in *Art, Conversation* and *Passion,* and most importantly for *Dreaming* of the possibilities.

Huge Love goes to my children, Rowan Delphius and Kahlil Hayden; who have made me a better man, inspired my creativity, and given me a reason to grow and expand who I am. **ONE**

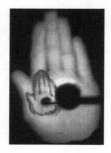

CONTENTS

Somewhere

"I see your eyes,
Up close and personal.
Always for the first time."
Julie Rae Carrigan

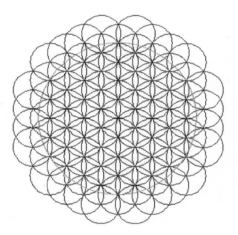

This Book Is Dedicated To
Julie Rae Carrigan
Your Poetry still beats in the hearts
of so many. You Are Dearly Missed
By all who knew you.

Somewhere In Southern Massachusetts On A Tuesday Night @ 10:03 P.M.

Time was like a giant raging river to Oscar Manchez as he stood at the door of the man's home, a man he'd been searching so many years to find. He was ready for the moment, he'd been dreaming of it for years, and was about to be rewarded for having never given up his quest.

Oscar's adrenaline spiked as he rang the doorbell. A long quiet moment went by where their seemed to be no response. So, Oscar pushed the doorbell button again, ringing it twice consecutively.

This time a moment later, the front porch's light turned on, and the doors locks could be heard being unbolted. When the door opened, a tall man with dark silvery hair and a very cruel look carved upon his wrinkled face, answered.

"What do want?!" with a grumpy huff of agitation the elder yelled at Oscar from his place in the doorway, trying to look intimidating.

It was not very effective, as the old man stood there wearing a red bathrobe with his hair uncombed, there was still a little shaving cream on his neck, and a slight trickle of blood from where his razor had cut him. He looked very frail now, weaker than Oscar had expected for a ruthless man of his renown, he'd not passed the years so gracefully, he'd aged more like a troll would, and had even started to resemble one slightly in the neon glow of the porch light. Age had gotten to him like mold upon a month old loaf of bread left in the fridge to rot. "What the hell do you want?!" said the troll in the doorway again.

Oscar had thought for years about all the things he'd say to this man, when this moment came, he'd filled endless notepads with imaginings of all the things he could say to a man such as this.

But when the moment had finally arrived, Oscar found he was ultimately speechless, and so abandoned all poetic dispositions, and instead got straight to the point.

With a quick whipping extension of Oscar's right arm, he sent his fist smashing into the old man's face, hitting him square on the nose and sending him falling flat onto his back as his red robe unfolded like a flower unfurling as he hit the ground, revealing the man's decrepit and wrinkled old body.

Oscar then let himself in and shut the door behind him.

"Wh—wh—why?" the words gurgled through blood and spit, bubbling with every gasp from the old man's mouth as he avoided looking up toward the intruder standing tall over him, like a vulture, staring him down with menacing eyes. "Wh-why?" He repeated.

"Why... That's what I used to ask myself about the sins that you committed upon me and mine." Oscar had no sympathy for this man; hell, he had little sympathy for anyone at all in fact. Even more, it was pleasing him very much to see this man now lying there in pain, laid out and broken.

"Diego Manchez is why..." Oscar tells the man flatly.

The old man finally managed to look Oscar in the eyes from his place on the floor; he was beginning to recover a blurry consciousness from the heavy fisted blow that Oscar had given him.

"I'm... I'm so sorry..." was all that the old man had to say.

"You'll never be sorry enough."

"I gave up that life, a long time ago, I'm a Mormon now. I-I found god an-"

"Shut up! I don't wann'ah hear your fucking sob story old man!..." Oscar stepped directly over the old man, pinning each of his hands under his boots, finger bones could be heard cracking in unison with the old man's gasps and cries.

"Where are your car keys?" Oscar asks.

The old man just cried, not answering.

Oscar decided to snatch his attention by grabbing his balls and squeezing them in his fist, the old man immediately regained his focus on what Oscar was saying.

"Where are the damned car keys?"

"*On – da... **Kitchen counter!...***"

Oscar finally let his grip go from the man's crotch and steps off his shattered hands, as he began to make his way over to the kitchen in the next room.

Oscar was a little disappointed at how weak the old man was; he was nowhere near the man

3

he'd been in his younger more ruthless days, as a mercenary running guns with Oscar's Father Diego Manchez.

Time had swelled all these years to here and now for them both, and the moment was to him like a raging river was about to break through the levees of history and smash through the Dam of injustice, a barrier that had haunted him all these years. *And Oscar was the raging floodwaters. He was the fury of nature unleashed*; Oscar was a man who'd never rested to find the men responsible for taking his Father from him so many years before.

Upon finding the car keys where he had said they were, Oscar then quickly made his way back toward the old man over near the front door, who was now slowly crawling on the floor, trying to make his way toward the living room off to his right.

The effort was futile, but Oscar slightly admired the fight still left in him. Nonetheless, his hatred took over as he kicked him in the ribs as hard as he could. The old man slumped to a fetus position, while lying in the puddle of his blood smeared upon the maple flooring, crying like a child.

"Listen old man, I know who you really are, and I know what you did to my Father..." Oscar bends down and grabs the man by his hair, ripping his head to face him down, eye to eye.

The old man is terrified; Oscar senses it in his shaking and darting eyes, blood splotching his face like a Jackson Pollack painting.

"It's time we set things right once and for all."

Oscar pulls from his belt harness a large knife, of which he puts its sharp tip directly in front of the old man's right eye.

The old man tries to pull back, but Oscar has a firm grip on his hair, and holds him steady, as he slowly pushes the knife into the socket.

No one in the neighborhood heard the old man's dying screams.

No one in the neighborhood saw Oscar drive away with the old man's car, and slip away into the night either; on his way towards *Route-One*.

Oscar's night was just beginning, for there was still one more man with whom he had a score to settle, and he was not going to let anything stop him from having his vengeance.

He was not that kind of man. Not at all.

He was the kind of man who had trained his whole life for this fateful night, a relentless and vigorous person; and a soldier who now only had one thing left to do.

Kill Desmond...

But before he could do that, Oscar was noticing that he would first have to stop somewhere for gas, since the old man's car was running on empty.

Northward on *Route-One* and into the night he drove, a man with a mission, heartless, as he'd been for so many years now, unaware that the road ahead - was stormy.

Somewhere Along The East Coast On Route-One
1:33 A.M.

Ponderings of the past, and contemplations of the future - was what was on the menu of his mind, as his car radio blared loudly the tune *Chan-Chan* by *The Buena Vista Social Club* as he drove northward on U.S. Route-One. Vang Cha's thoughts were floating like clouds. As he watched the violent lightning storm brewing over the Atlantic Ocean approaching the Eastern shoreline to his right, his mind was absorbed by the static energy of the ominous night ahead; he still had a long ways to drive before he would be at his destination.

But it's the journey that counts, as they say.

The young man, twenty-two years of age according to his driver's license, was steering a very beat up old *Ford Gran Torino* with a faded-green paint job, and was currently embarked on a very ancient shamanistic family ritual called a *Hu Plig*--or as he would say in English, a *'Soul Calling'*.

This tradition had been a part of Vang's clan's spiritual practice for several thousand years, and consisted of a male shaman praying and making a *'calling out'* to every *'wandering soul'* in the family, and to all the ancestors and spirits; to unite the Kin for a very large family gathering. And being modern times the *'sage'* would even use a *telephone* to make some of these *'calls'*, for practical purposes of course.

Most people when they saw him just thought him *Asian – usually thinking Japanese or Chinese.* But in fact, if you so cared to actually know, Vang Cha would proudly tell you that he was *Hmong,* and was making his way homeward on what was essentially a good old-fashioned family reunion - which he very much looked forward to and enjoyed celebrating. The whole extended family, all several hundred of them, would gather once a year to feast for several days and play music, eat lots of food and celebrate their life.

A '*Soul Calling*' was now quite a modern event, actually, and the conversations at the *Hu Plig* for the Cha clan gathering ran the whole gamut of topics for anyone living life in the 21st century. All his elders, aunts, uncles and cousins, and second, and third, and fourth cousins, all spoke about such subjects as sports, politics, and global warming, SAT studies, the newest cell phone apps available, or what the funniest videos on *YouTube* at the moment were- a*nd the ever expanding use and need of the Internet in our daily lives.* These were all issues of deep concern to them in their day-to-day lives, just as they were for everyone else, most everywhere around the world these days, it seemed.

His ethnic culture, being orally based, was especially fragile and fading away. *Such is the plight of all tribal peoples everywhere*, he thought sadly. Vang's family were really no different from most anyone else's in America; save one thing - they were *recent* immigrants to the *United States,* and still proudly knowledgeable and thickly rooted in their cultural heritage of their ancestry. His parents and grandparents could still remember the world before the days of strip malls and traffic jams, and suburban gentrification.

America was made up and populated almost *completely* of immigrants after all, besides the few scattered Native American clans that had managed to survive the holocaust of the European, Chinese and African onslaughts of people that swarmed the Eastern Seaboard of North America starting in the 1500's.

To be Hmong - Vang thought wasn't too different than being a tribal Native American. His people had been wandering the lands of South East Asia long before the time of modern governments, and their imaginary Borders that gave the lands names such as *Vietnam, Thailand, Laos, Burma* or *Myanmar* and *China.*

So often Vang found himself being asked during parties at College about his cultural roots, but the conversation would often eventually then veer quickly back towards *American pop culture*, at the other drunken person's insistence of course – the person usually being too embarrassed that they were completely unfamiliar with his ethnic history.

When Vang found himself in a situation like this, and it happened often since he was living the *'dorm life'* in his Freshman year at college now, he would just smile and politely go along with the segue; not wanting to force his culture upon them. He would then joyfully join in dialogue with the person about more familiar topics, not wanting to appear out of touch with his upbringing as an American.

Such was the life of being an immigrant.

But Vang had found, especially in college, that a lot of people actually were sincerely interested in learning more about his *Hmong* heritage, and he would have the opportunity to share a bit about the beautiful and ancient history of his people, about their spiritual practices of shamanistic guidance, and their strong almost fervent sense of family and honor that made up his rich culture.

But that was the past, a past he was struggling to hold onto, within this *uber*-hip present day fast food society called *American life*.

To really have a discussion about what it was like to be *Hmong* would be a very lengthy and heated conversation. The same could happen if you were to ask what it was to be an *American*; the answers would be varied and jaded by individual geographical differences.

Vang had long deduced that the world's differences were quickly melting away into a stew called *'Globalization'* and the battle to hold onto our individual identity was a struggle everyone on the planet had in common with each other now.

'How little most Americans really know about their own roots and history anymore - let alone any other peoples' his Grandfather had often remarked - Lee Cha, who was a man who'd fought in wars, survived death squads, and who had traveled all over the world, before he had repatriated to America. Where most Americans couldn't name more than a dozen or so Presidents' names, his Grandfather, a man not even born in the states, could name them all, in order, and even tell you which political parties they had heralded from.

The concept around present day global culture, disappointingly, Vang had found mainly seemed to try and narrow the world's ethnic heritage by classifying us - *All Seven Billion and counting* – simply into just a few major classes of peoples or races. Which were, simply put: *White/ American/ European, Black /African, Latino/ Spanish, Jewish, Arab, Asian, Persian, Native American and Aboriginal.*

It was an apparent social mentality he'd been tolerating his entire life, having been born and raised in the Unites States of America.

However, Vang wasn't at a loss of American friends who were interested and experienced in his cultural ways. Vang had already become painfully aware that it seemed many Americans sometimes just didn't care to know much about other people, their places and ways. And even if they did care, the story of his family's journey to America was filled with such grand hardship and bravery, which few Americans could even come close to relating to. So, like most kids he rarely tried to relate, and sought to fit in...

Vang remembered reading about the Amish in high school, who still lived their lives without the use of technology; he was fascinated by the fact that right there smack-dab in the middle of Pennsylvania was a large population of people still going at it the good old-fashioned way, similar to his ancestors still living in Asia.

Maybe the *Amish* were *Refugees themselves* from the ever-encroaching *world of high technology* surrounding us all, which appeared to his grandfather to permeate every aspect of life now so completely *'That we seemed to be forgetting who we really are'.*

Vang was also keenly aware that the entire world seemed to be one giant cauldron of human stew swirling further and further into a-state of cultural homogenization and entropy, which his clan was slowly melting away into. The entropy of culture could be called *Mass Media*, or *Consumerism*, or any other of a thousand terms. *It really does not matter what you call it; it is all just mass confusion,* he thought to himself. Vang wondered if technology was turning everyone, all of us, the entire world, over into 'cultural Exiles?'

What if modern media were gentrifying our minds in what perhaps could be called a *'thought holocaust'?* Turning us all into refugees from the Tsunami of *modern industrial thinking* that was paving the world over, and eating and gobbling up the earth's resources so quickly and unsustainably, all while most watched their hypnotic screens, oblivious.

All in the name of *'quarterly profits'* and *'Progress'.* He was haunted by the thought of a ravaged world that his children might inherit if things kept hurtling as they were – t*owards a cliff with no breaks*.

Vang suddenly mused to himself wondering which science fiction book or movie will have successfully predicted what the world would look like fifty years from now.

Would it be like *BladeRunner* or *Mad Max?* Would it be like *Children of Men* or a *Brave New World*? How much will the world change in the next generation now that Technology was speeding up the pace of everything?

Vang's family knew well how much could change in just a generation or two; it had been just two generations between Vang's gadget filled existence in America and his family's very simple and tribal based way of life in the Jungle Mountains of Asia. *What if?* Vang wondered; *modern advertisements* and *mainstream media* and *24 hour news cycles* filled with a constant barrage of needs and gossip, had all just become one behemoth *'thought virus'* which was spreading apathy and indifference like *Spam* and *Malware* through our minds, through all of us, *Everywhere - the whole world over?*

Vang Cha understood from his life experience that the unique cultural identities of all people everywhere - white, black, brown, yellow, purple, hell even the pink and blue -peoples the world over were being marginalized in this modern existence.

All of our personal cultural identities were being uprooted and paved over, and no one was safe from the bulldozer.

Natural forests and farms, villages and streams, have been replaced by billboard advertising, strip malls echoing meaningless yet catchy pop music in concrete jungles, and the only escape is an occasional 3-D movie, or video game with little redeeming value to us as human beings.

They all seemed to be selling everyone the same thing: *An impossible dream,* Vang lamented. The modern world, not just America, but every nation of the world, seemed a throw-away-culture that was trashing our collective future's true potential, all in the name of a fleeting financial profit that only benefited a few, and only momentarily.

Vang thought how nice it would be to live an impossible adventure like in the movies; to find a real princess of his own and save her, while getting rich doing so... *And he would be happy if it didn't involve him having to kill anyone too.* The thought brought a smile to his face. How nice it would be if fairytales like that *actually came true* in this life. At least the good and happy ones, unlike some, which were very - *Grimm* indeed.

Vang's family knew well what *grim* was, more than most - and the effects that political and social entropy could have on life.

Being refugees from their homelands.

The *Hmong* people had been repatriating to America since the end of the *Vietnam War*. His clan had for decades during the war put their lives, and often times, even their entire cultural existence at risk helping the American soldiers fight the communists. After the fall of *Laos* in early May of '75 to the *Communist Party*, many of Vang Cha's people had been recruited and trained by the *CIA* to fight as soldiers.

The *Hmong* people were, simply put, *proxy* soldiers, used in what was called *'the secret war'* and they had been pivotal in helping the U.S. military block the *Ho Chi Minh Trail* of supplies and munitions to the *Viet Cong*. They had endangered their villages and families' lives helping countless numbers of pilots who had been shot down make their way to safety when they had found themselves caught behind enemy lines in a very hostile Laotian Panhandle.

The *Hmong* people were called *freedom fighters* back then, and were showered with weapons and assistance, to fight *communism* for the American people.

But today his people are called *refugees*, and were forced essentially to beg for assistance from the very government that they had sacrificed so much for. Many of his people to this day were still being persecuted in Asia for assisting the US Government, who conveniently would like to forget all about them, it seemed sometimes.

And yet, the very men and their families who sacrificed so much for this country years ago - since *9/11* and the *War on Terror* under the new *Patriot Act* laws - were being denied Political Asylum.

Many *Hmong 'freedom fighters'* who had been praised by *CIA* directors as some of the biggest heroes of the Vietnam conflict were now ironically considered potentially hostile and dangerous to the very government that trained them in the ways of war in the first place.

After the fall of Saigon in early may of 1975, the Hmong people were targeted by the communists who took control of Laos and told that they would be exterminated *'to the last root'* as revenge for their cooperation with American forces during the Vietnam War. That's what had forced his family and people to flee their tribal homelands, evacuated by just a few planes and helicopters in a very desperate flight from fast approaching death squads.

Vang reflected about the few times that his family members had talked at length how against all odds they pulled the resources together to attempt a mass exodus of their family and other mostly Hmong people to safety. Several men, among them Hmong leaders, and a few CIA case Officers, who had been the only Americans remaining in Long Tieng at the time, organized a desperate exodus. They had daringly stripped a small fleet of aircraft of their national markings, as the mission at the time was ironically considered an *illegal act of war?* Imagine that: after all the bloodshed and carnage, at the end of it all they define one of the major humanitarian events an act of war - for sending them in to rescue as many people as they could.

His Grandfather always called it '*the massive flock of copters and planes*' that had come for them all; he would recount how they raged across the Laotian panhandle and swooped into hostile territory for one reason, to save as many lives as humanly possible.

Vang had heard the stories several times, and *every time* it still managed to fill him with a creepy kind of awe - of how close his entire family had actually come to being extinguished from this planet.

Vang imagined what it had been like for his father and mother, as they were being shot at, while trying to escape their homes. He tried to envision what it would have felt like to be aboard a huge helicopter flying over the sea, low on fuel and well past their recommended capacity, with twice as many people as the machine was built to carry.

His mother had *literally* tossed Vang's older brother out of a helicopter – only to be miraculously caught by an American navy officer on the deck of an overburdened aircraft carrier. Vang's mother then had been forced to jump a hundred feet into a frigid sea to escape the failing gravity of the fuel-less machine that was being flown by his uncle, who struggled to the bitter end to hover the massive failing Huey helicopter long enough for everyone to evacuate. Before crashing it into the water safely away from the ship, where he died instantly a heartbroken hero.

The pullout was so ill-planned and desperate, and the sheer numbers of evacuees so vast, and the threat of genocide so dire, that an entire fleet of helicopters and planes was scrapped to the deep abyss of the ocean, to save as many of his people as possible that day. Yet the goal hadn't been just humanitarian based, more importantly to the generals, anyways, the fleet needed to be scrapped in order to keep the technology out of the hands of the enemies. Vang remembered he had seen some old news footage of men pushing a helicopter off the deck of an aircraft carrier and into the depths of the ocean, to make way for more landings. That had been them; fleeing the place they'd called home for thousands of years – and if that hadn't been tragic enough, many of his family had watched as their friends and family were gunned down as they fled their villages in haste.

The day his clan was forced to leave their homeland began an odyssey that was *'a mixed journey of extremes.'* His Grandfather had told him that it had been filled with such tragedy and heartbreak, while at the same time bounding with some of the greatest moments of human compassion that he'd remembered ever witnessing.

Vang often marveled at how close his entire family had come to being executed. He reflected about the countless stories of brave sacrifice he'd heard recounted; the death of a family member in many cases had come when they'd chosen to stay and fight off the approaching death squads, allowing the others to escape to freedom and survive. The Cha Clan alone had lost hundreds of people altogether since the Vietnam War had begun. Over the following years, tens of thousands of his people have made their way to Thailand as refugees from his homelands. And though it might not be as heated as it was in the nineteen-seventies, his people were still being persecuted to this day in their native lands.

Vang was thoroughly aware of the cold hard reality of this world. He knew this life wasn't a faery tale. That in this world of *globalization*, and *IMF's* and *World Banks* with their so-called *'Fairtrade?'* – that, well - often the bad guys won; horrible people have tremendous power and wealth today, and the true heroes of our world usually went unnoticed, and frequently unrewarded for their sacrifices, or even worse, treated as hostiles or imprisoned and killed.

His peoples had been left to a very *grim* plight at the end of the Vietnam War. Vang suddenly wondered which came first, the word *Grim*, or the name *Grimm*?

Something he knew that he would *Wikipedia* next chance he got, his toes tapping with the rhythm of the Cabaña music playing on his beat up old cassette deck on his dashboard. The music was all scratched up and faded, and half the sounds of the original recording had faded away, but his imagination filled in the holes, knowing the song well.

Vang wondered where this *'great American compassion'* his grandfather had often spoken about *had gone?* Having not witnessed much of the older generation's idea of *'Compassion'* to the extent that it was so hyped, he wished that there were still more of it left. The America he'd witnessed and grown up in was the America of hidden racism and culture shock, with violent *Street Gangs,* crack ravaged city dwellings with under-funded and crumbling schools – all while the wealthy at the same time were robbing everyone blind, wealthier than ever before.

Yet, if you watched the news at all, it always seemed that the biggest enemies were ironically the poorest of us. Even though Corporations and an elite class of the wealthiest Americans were literally, and often illegally, not paying their fair share of taxes - equaling in the hundreds of billions of dollars if not trillions – annually every year, it seemed the few billion a year that went toward helping our needy children and elders, or our wounded war veterans, were the causes of our social ills and deemed by the idiot box to be the supposed *"enemy of our nations fiscal stability"?..*

At least to the *weapon of mass distraction* that passes for *'News'* these days, filled with 'expert talking heads' with their ten-second sound bites. Vang at this moment wondered what type of *ethics class* the journalists of today had taken in college, if any at all? Because the way they did, their *'info-tainment'* news was downright scary and almost ethnically racist, it seemed these days.

Growing up a foreigner in America he'd lost count of how many times he'd been told to just *'go home'* by another ignorant, and usually white, American child - who'd usually be wearing army surplus clothing and would also make other ignorant comments like *'my daddy fought your kind in Vietnam to protect our freedoms!'* of all things, to add insult to injury.

Go home?!? He would want to scream at them. *I can't go home. If we were to go home, my 'kind' would be executed for having fought to protect your ignorant daddy's freedoms in Vietnam you Jackass!*

War just leaves everything shattered and empty... Vang mulled. Then looking down at his fuel gauge realized so too was his gas tank. He had stopped monitoring the fuel gauge for sometime now, but now was realizing that he was in dire need of fuel and began to hope that a fill up station was not to far ahead.

Lightning made the sky glow and flicker, and a misting rain began to dart his windshield; rumbling and crackling thunder joined the soundtrack of the Cuban tune playing as Vang turned his wipers on, adding more ambient rhythmic 'swishing' sound to the mood music of the moment while he drove north.

While thinking of the consumer society that he was living in Vang Cha saw a large lit billboard sign ahead, on which was a very creepy looking moose-man announcing that there was a twenty-four hour gas station just a few miles up the road in a town called Ashton.

As he drove toward the town he'd never heard of, he was able to look out over the dark expansive horizon, and see the flashing fury of the approaching storm; the scenes soundtrack was his dusty old Gran Torino engine and his tires humming steadily, and rhythmically, over the large Steele bridge.

His *Soul Calling* journey was taking him through Maine for the first time, and he was sad that he was only passing through during the middle of the night, and wouldn't be able to see more of the area and its people.

Like most, he was completely unaware of life's sudden detour awaiting ahead.

1:42 A.M.

People only stopped at **Conway's Quikee** for three basic human needs, and it was the immediate desire for these products which had allowed a dinosaur store like *Conway's* to still survive in the battled economy of a global world, with their big box stores and their low-low prices, and million dollar ad campaigns.

The *three needs* that kept Rowan painfully employed and desperately under paid were *Alcohol, Tobacco, and Gas.* If people were in dire necessity of any of these three items, then they might find themselves inclined to stop in.

If not, then they just kept driving past.

Most of the families in the surrounding area had long since begun to shop at all the larger corporate stores up north or south of Ashton, abandoning the local run-down stores like Conway's Gas Depot, in exchange for the shiny-bling of large box stores.

Though everyone around town still pretended that they lived out in the boondocks, they all knew that the city was creeping slowly toward them.

'Not fast enough' Rowan thought to herself.

The twenty-four hour gas station and convenience store was the only thing open for miles around, at least past sunset anyways. That is the way it had always been in Ashton, or as far as she could remember.

The sign on the store that Rowan Ellian worked at read **CONWAY'S QUIKEE GAS DEPOT & SNACK SHACK** and was accompanied by a very tacky and obscenely wacky looking cartoon moose-man character, which had an almost sinister grin upon its face.

20

And as if the Cartoon logo were not already bugged-out enough by its very shoddy rendering, the moose-man was also schizophrenically drinking a beer and smoking a cigarette, as he was also loaded up with junk food in one arm while gassing up his hummer with the other.

Rowan Ellian, with all her twenty- one years of angst and spunk, had one major problem; She was bored as hell, and helplessly enduring yet another red-eye shift on a job that was taking her *nowhere.*

Rowan had been realizing for some time now that her life had no real surprises in store for her.

Or at least, that's what Rowan thought.

Being the store's full time night shift cashier and gas attendant had been starting to takes its toll on her. A certain melancholy numbness was now tapping her normally bubbly, and most would say charming, personality. Others had been noticing it too.

Like her mother, who had just the day before mentioned that maybe it would be nice if she found a nice boy and settled down.

As if there were any *'nice desirable men'* anywhere to be found in these parts of the woods. Or even on the planet for that matter?

She reckoned, *'trying to find a nice guy ah'round here is like trying to find a beaver in the desert',* as her grandmother would have put it, before she died. Rowan would always just ignore the old woman's sayings and advice, but perhaps she *was* right after all. Maybe a beaver had a better chance of building a dam in the desert than she did of finding true love...

She was slightly disturbed by the sudden realization of how often she found her

Grandmother's wisdom to ring true the older she got.

She then decided that she needed to reflect on something a bit more youthful, and thought about the few boys who had sparked her passions and ignited her heart aflutter, making her feel more alive and less lonely.

There were Allen, Joey, and of course *Tony*.

She then painfully remembered how all of them just as quickly broke her heart, by either moving away or getting with another woman.

Rowan tried to imagine what it would be like to live life being desired by lovely men, like in all those smut magazines lining the walls. Or, what if she got a gig being a rich man's wife, with all those toys and liberties and credit cards. But then she wasn't so sure that she even wanted that, thinking she also would have to deal with all the stress and glorious debt that comes with such a life, and probably end up with a man like her boss Carl Conway in the end.

The very thought of being with a man like Carl sent shivers down Rowan's spine.

Best stop that train of thought, she concluded.

Rowan was born and bred in Ashton, and found it a nice enough place to grow up, she would admit that much, but now that she was an adult, it was starting to appear very dull to her. Every street and beachfront was the same old thing she had seen for way too long. She was uninspired by her life, and desperately in need of change, though she was at a loss as to how she could escape the rut called her life.

Rowan's uniform would have been comfortable enough to wear, if it were not so rudely embarrassing to be seen dressed in, as it was a shameless extension of the ridiculous *'Quikee'* theme, and what it implied. With the *moose's antler rack* placed on the shirt directly over her *breast rack,* which to Rowan's dismay welcomed every pervert in the surrounding three counties to leave a comment or two about.

Rowan was often thoroughly amazed that in a world where things seemed so homogenized, people were still finding new and creative ways to be rude with each other. She was thrown constantly by the uniform into situations which forced her to comprehend how many of the moronic creeps, who to her suffering made up a good portion of the store's clientele, so often truly believed they were being cute when acting this way, too.

Men are so dense, Rowan thought to herself.

As if she were not already awkward enough with her own existence to begin with, the whole creepy moose shirt thing definitely added to the discomfort of her life. Particularly when it was a nightly torture, which she had endured for eight, and even sometimes ten and twelve, hours a night, between the hours of eleven P.M. and seven A.M. For six days a week she'd done so, for almost three lamentable years now.

But, Rowan was the kind of woman that always tried desperately to make the best of any situation. Especially the ones you are stuck dealing with. And, though the shirt was embarrassing, she still managed to make it work for her in a laid-back kind of way.

Her hair was often a little disheveled from the busy nature of her job, but she didn't really much care if her hair wasn't always perfect looking.

Rowan wasn't completely void of fashion sense, though some had claimed otherwise; she was never much caught up with the fancy modern girl look, and had a certain grace to her unique personal taste in the way she dressed and groomed. She was not into makeup, nor did she have any heavy obsession with how she looked at *all* times.

Like her mother, who was so obsessed with how she looked and how others perceived her, that she literally took two hours getting dressed just to walk the hundred feet to the mailbox at the end of the driveway, *right outside of her very own house.* God forbid a neighbor dare get a glimpse of her not looking perfect.

Rowan wondered why her mother acted as if she were some hot young Hollywood starlet scared that the paparazzi would get a glimpse of her in a moment of normalness. *As if it were some sort of image kryptonite to be seen* not *looking like Martha Stewart?*

Rowan for some time already had come to terms with the fact that her parents would never make any sense to her. Trying to understand her family, she found, *was like trying to fly to the moon with a bicycle*; good luck with that!

Now this particular *carefree* personality trait, which Rowan embraced in her dress code and attitude, only adding to her already charmingly cute demeanor (though she was unaware of it) made her a very attractive and desirable woman to most men, young and old. Having the voluptuous sweetness of the whole girl-next-door aura to her, she was hardly short of opportunities with men.

Although all the older creeps and local Perverts wanting her attention bothered Rowan, she knew how to handle them. It was however she discovered, the lack of confidence with the younger men, and her complete inability to manage herself smoothly around them, that really troubled her most.

Rowan sighed a mixed exclamation of desire and hopelessness, as she looked upon an ancient clock on the store's wall. It declared the time to be 1:43.

She swore it was cursed; Rowan really believed that this clock in particular seemed *always* to defy the usual laws of time and space by moving slower than humanly bearable. And it did so, oddly enough, only when she was working.

The clock, like almost everything else in the store, was a thing from the era before the digital revolution took over the world. Except for the security camera system and the computer operated scanner cash register, the place was filled with the feeling of what all of the Town – hell, the whole state - had once upon a time been like; tired looking and dusty.

Even the citizens of an *'east-bum-fuck'* town like Ashton were all linked into the frenzied modern bustle now. The very same people who had often joked that Ashton was *'far from the city and close to nowhere!'* just a few years before, were all a part of the world of technological wonders now, itching to get their hands on the next digital marvel that was on sale at the big box stores. Farmers and anglers alike all were now driving around with their satellite connected smart phone, receiving Internet in the middle of the woods.

Rowan was *so* tired of all the old-timers commenting about how much *'things have changed'* since they were kids. Conversations consisting of *Back in the good old days when they were killing Indians and walking 50 thousand miles to school barefoot with a thousand pounds of books and rocks on their backs,* and what not, were almost single handedly boring her to death, and they would just go on and on about it forever, it seemed.

Like a never-ending conversation with one of those talking and singing mantle fish you could get at all the trinket shops, she thought, push a button and the thing said the same four or five things, and nothing else. Rowan recalls with whimsy all those novelty singing fish toys in their boxes, shaking their cold and frigid plastic bodies while dancing to the cheesy techno beats, crooning popular 90's sex tunes to cheap karaoke music. *Just like many of her customers,* she thought. 'Cheap, and definitely *Not TOO Sexy'*...

'No shit', she would want to scream at them every time, but of course wouldn't. *'It's quite obvious everything has changed!'*

She needed to hear one more old-timer reminding her of how much things have changed as much as she needed another migraine headache, which Conway's store lighting tended to give her, and were often triggered by stories of old-timers, oddly enough. It probably wouldn't be so bad if it were not for the fact that almost all the longwinded tales of *how much life had changed* seemed to involve a lot of *fondling* a five hundred dollar phone with their grimy hands, and her breasts with their yearning eyes.

She wondered if the phone fondling was an attempt to look younger and hip. Or if it was a way of trying to flaunt whatever wealth they *usually didn't* have? But then she wondered if this 'trick' ever really worked for them with younger girls - then decided she really didn't care what the answer was.

Nowadays it was 3-D movies, and singing robot fish, that excited the world of mass consumers, and most certainly not creepy moose-man characters; of this she was sure.

Rowan thought to herself about how nice it would be to own a robot. She imagined how great it would be to have it do all the work for her.

Or, even perhaps a clone would be best, she concluded. She suddenly wondered what porn in 3-D would be like. Then she smiled at the absurdity of all those ideas.

She found herself smiling at the wishes and dreams of adventure that she often spent so many hours, days, weeks – *hell, years* now - thinking about.

How nice it would be if she were able to just up-and-quit this forsaken job, finally travel, and have some real adventures. Rowan wanted desperately to see more of the world, or go to college, or just do *anything* besides spend her life stuck at *Conway's Quikee Gas Depot*.

Anything-anything-anything!

'Anything at all!!!' She screamed inside her head, staring at the dreadful clock.

Anything at all would be just fine, as long as it was far away from Ashton.

She then wondered about having all the wealth of a man like her boss, Carl Conway, who was probably the richest guy in the whole surrounding area, and most probably the biggest sleaze-ball too.

Rowan kept wanting to believe that good people get rich as well, though she was having trouble remembering ever meeting any exceptionally nice wealthy people, people like that she guessed had no interest in a shit-hole-town such as hers.

No, the types of people who gravitated into the black hole of Ashton tended to be, well, more shady, like the king sleaze, her boss. Carl Conway, though married, *and somehow* well respected amongst most of the town folk, had been trying to get into her pants since before she was even legal.

Rowan was sharp though, and knew how to handle men like him; having been raised in a town filled with predators, she was well versed in the ways with which a woman should handle wild beasts.

It's like being a 'Lion-Tamer', she thought, as a memory of her childhood moved forward into her mind. It was of when she met a real-life Lion-Tamer with her grandfather at the circus, so many years ago; the man said to her: *'When one is found to be in the cage with the beast, you mustn't show the Lion that you're afraid. Otherwise they will smell that fear; and eat you.'*

It was the same with people like Carl, she thought; *you mustn't let them know you're scared.*

Rowan had come to know that men like him almost seemed to get off on fear; it turned them on in some morbidly primal way. She guessed that's why Carl so much enjoyed all those Hollywood Horror films he rented all the time.

In Rowan's opinion, these were nothing more than legalized snuff films, which she rarely wasted her time ever watching.

Rowan had discovered years before that when a girl acts with a certain kind of 'take no shit' attitude, and could successfully *'laugh it off through bitching'* to the sordid suitor, she could then usually just end up reminding the slime-ball of his wife, or even worse, his *Mother in Law*.

It was sort of like anti-Viagra to do that, she had found.

She was good at it, too, and it usually worked well enough for her to get by in a place like Ashton.

Rowan decided immediately that she would forever forth coin that strategy the *'Mother in Law Effect'*.

She then realized, with a depressed sigh, that she might be *too* good at such a strategy. That it just might have kept all the nice desirable men away as well.

She then nervously laughed the thought away. Desperately hoping such a notion couldn't at all be true. She knew that there must be a wonderful man out there - *somewhere*, wanting to love her, and be loved by her. *Right?*

She then had a scary vision of herself as a lonely old woman living with an army of cats, ranting about *'how much things have changed...'*
She shivered.

Rowan sighed as she stared up at the old and tawdry clock on the wall, wondering what the future had *in-store*; or hopefully for her *out*-of-this-godforsaken-*store*...

As the time was now declaring a sarcastic, and very depressing, time of **1:44** to her.

"Close enough" she said aloud to herself about the time, knowing that Carl wouldn't like that she was taking another break several hours before her next *scheduled* one.

Nor would Mr. Conway appreciate that she had a small habit of *sneaking* Snicker bars every once in a while, as a part of her as of yet *non-existent pay raise.*

But Carl wasn't there, and being a self–liberating-feminist - and also an indentured servant - concluded she certainly could do as she pleased when he wasn't around; she certainly felt as if she had earned it, even if a man like Carl was too greedy to give her a raise after all these years of loyal service.

So. Grabbing her sinful delight, she made her way outside for some fresh air, ripping the Snickers packaging as if she had no patience for it being in the way, then began devouring the candy inside, as she escaped through the service entrance and out into the nights tempestuous air.

On the horizon above the tree line there is a flash of lightning which draws Rowan's attention, and she watches with sudden amazement as it sizzles across the sky. Then is immediately followed by a booming crackle of thunder that rolls across the clouds in a very dominant declaration of the storms approach.

The thunderstorm was pushing its way from the east, coming in off the ocean '*As fierce as a sailors thirst for whisky*' as Grandma Elian would have said.

The wind quickly picked up its pace, tussling her hair. Rowan loved stormy nights like these. Something about them just filled her with a natural sense of awe, they reminded her of how powerfully vast and beautiful the world really was.

Rowan's synapses sparked in symphonic resonance with the random flashes of furious light in the sky above, as she now dreamed of visiting cities all over the world, and far away countries. 'China would be cool, or even Australia' she thought to herself, yet knew she was further away from affording such a dream than the actual places themselves were.

Another flashing discharge of lightning danced across the sky, triggering Rowan to marvel at something she remembered hearing on the radio several years before.   Supposedly lightning is hotter than the surface of the sun itself, when it strikes the ground. How do they know this stuff, she wondered, but wasn't able to journey with the thought for long, as her peaceful snickers break was shattered by the simultaneous arrival of four vehicles.

The first car, a nice older but well kept Cadillac, held a bickering elderly couple. As they exited their vehicle, so too did their dispute, for everyone to hear. "Mac and cheese should be baked!   Baked is the only way to go Henry. *Baked!*"

The second car, a very expensive black BMW, parked at fueling pump number three and was packed with several college kids around Rowan's age, three guys and a girl, none of whom Rowan was very interested in talking with.

Being that one of them was an ex-boyfriend.

Tony Sycamore and his *'dumbtourage'*, as she called them, begin to chuckle at this loud elderly woman yelling, *"Baked is the only way to go!"* Rowan didn't need to know the kids to guess they were probably all *baked* themselves.

Henry impatiently retorted, "How many times do I have to tell you Margaret? I like mine soft and gooey with the melted cheese sauce over the fresh pasta, *and not baked!*"

"How many times you gotta tell me? As many times as it takes for you to finally shut up about it, and get used to the way *I* make it. *That's how many...*"

The third vehicle to enter Conway's lot was a large pick-up truck that pulls in along side pump number four. Rowan knew who the truck belonged to right away, and found that, just as she suspected might be the case, a very drunk and aggressive Murdock Johnson, a man in his early forties wearing a cowboy hat, stumbled from the vehicle and began fueling up his truck.

Rowan could tell that Murdock was annoyed that he must listen to the elderly couple's squabble. She then was at a loss to remember a time when Murdock's mood wasn't annoyed. She never liked the unscrupulous man and always got a super creepy feeling every time he was around.

"I don't like my Mac and Cheese dried out and over cooked, and that crunchy topping you put on it. It mucks up my dentures, for god's sakes, Margaret." Henry declared.

The fourth car was Vang's Gran Torino.

Rowan, when she glimpsed him, instantly thought that he was a fairly attractive young Asian man, as she watched him pop the hood on his antiquated yet still fashionable vehicle, to check the oil.

The stranger instantly intrigued Rowan; she could tell by the way he carried himself that the young man was her type. Rowan watched as Vang's attention, like everyone's, was suddenly drawn to the commotion being stirred by the elderly pair.

"You can have it any way you want - that is, if you wanna cook for yourself..." Margaret assured Henry, who called her bluff by proudly saying, "Fine! *Then* I will make my own..."

"I've been married to you for over thirty years. Trust me; I know you are not going to cook a damned thing," said Margaret, finding his bluff laughable.

The 'dumbtourage' - Tony, Scott and 'Tiny' - were busy trying to impress the sassy girl with very immature masculine antics and buffoonery to care any more about the couple bickering. And to Rowan's dismay and intense agitation, the young vixen was eating up all the attention, smiling at all the boys' flirtation.

Suddenly the girl looked over towards Rowan and made eye contact with her.

Rowan found herself giving the girl a viperous look of a woman scorned, while trying to remember her name.

Finding Rowan's awkward attempt at an evil eye amusing, the girl began to pat her hair proudly, as she began fueling up her fabulous BMW with daddy's credit card.

Lisa – something? Trying to remember the girl's last name.

She had met Lisa at Perkins Peer out at the old Oakledge overlook park area, during a party the year before.

She knew that her family had a vacation home in the area, and that her father made a lot of money in banking, or something or other high stakes and high class, down south in one of the large cities.

She also recalled that the girl *'wasn't the brightest bulb in the socket'*, as her grandmother would have put it. Rowan recalled being stunned that this girl, who, by *her own admission,* barely passed high school, was now attending one of them fancy *Ivy-league colleges!* On something she had called a 'legacy scholarship', which was just a nice way of saying *'I'm stinking **Rich!**'* She felt resentment as *'Jersey Girl'* was all proud and self-righteous, and the center of these boys' very bubbled world...

Rowan was adamant that a girl like Lisa would never have made it into her prestigious college of choice, if it were not for daddy's spectacular *'legacy'* and money.

This in particular is what most infuriated Rowan about the girl Lisa. Trying to imagine how Grandma Elian would have said it if she were still around, imagining it might go something like *'Just goes to show that just because you can buy an education doesn't mean that you can buy intelligence'* Rowan thought snidely.

Rowan knew that she would still be in college, if only she could afford it. Even her good grades, and the few grants and college loans she had managed to pull together after high school couldn't even *come close* to covering the enormous cost of tuition at any college worth attending.

She knew this because she had tried.

For half a year she had attended the local state university and did smashingly well, that is until the money ran out. She was then forced to retreat back to Ashton, broke, and into this job she now so much loathed.

Rowan tried so desperately hard to escape this town, but still ended up at Conway's anyway. This job was supposed to be her serious attempt to *'Save some money to go back to school,'* as she had put it three years prior.

Her wages being what they were, Rowan would never be able to afford to get back to school, that she had already decided, after calculating it mathematically a thousand times already. The dream of higher education had been beyond her reach financially for some time now.

This saddened Rowan greatly, for she knew that if given the right opportunity she could prove she was capable of so much more than –well, just working at Conway's.

Rowan didn't care if she was judging the girl too harshly, and knew that she probably would even like Lisa given a chance to get to know her better, which unfortunately wasn't going to be today, given that she was hanging with her ex, Tony.

She knew, and didn't care, that she was jealous of Lisa's pampered good looks and carefree casualness in the way she spent loads of daddy's money.

Rowan deeply wished she was the one with the life of entitlement, and was not impressed that the girl seemed to be taking her privilege for granted. Nor was she surprised that such a damsel would be hanging with the 'Dumbtourage'.

Rowan's moment of people watching was interrupted as a fifth vehicle, a gas guzzling pickup truck driven by her sleazy boss, Carl Conway, drove in and parked near the entrance to the store. Carl immediately looked over, saw that she was taking an unscheduled break, and gave her a look of contempt.

"Great," said Rowan, who was tired of being humiliated for a job that didn't even give her a livable wage; but knew that it was all she had.

So, regrettably, she began to make her way back inside the store to service the onslaught of customers rapidly headed her way.

Tony's gang of idiots were the first ones to enter the store behind her. They immediately began grabbing munchies of all kinds, continuing the asinine behavior, which Rowan guessed probably started when their mothers decided to have children with creepy moose-men.

Rowan had a feeling that Tony wanted to rub in the fact that he was hanging with the cool rich girl now, instead of a dork like her.

As if breaking her heart at their friend AJ's party six months previous, *by leaving her for that whore Diane*, wasn't enough of a fuck you to her gullible pride.

It was small town nastiness like this that really got her most irritable, and inspired the strong desire of leaving her dead beat hometown, more than anything else - more than her shit job, or the same tired faces, with the same drained things to say, day after day after *fracking* day.

No! Something inside her screamed, trying to stop the boiling turmoil that was building up within her.

I will face this debacle with a more mature attitude, she told herself. She would rise above the childish antics of Tony's need to mess with her, of that she was certain.

Because she was *better than that, than him...*

Rowan took a deep breath as she abashedly wo-manned the helm of her cash register.

She was *ready for anything Tony was going to throw at her.*

At least, that's what she wanted to believe.

Every ounce of calm she had gathered watching the rain clouds brewing in the sky during her Snickers break was now being replaced by the emotional storm cloud that was snidely approaching her with a swagger of a man who's got nothing better to do than venom to speak, and ego to reap.

In the two months that Rowan had spent *going with* Tony, she had become very aware that his need to boost his ego off other peoples suffering was akin to a junkie's need to get high.

She certainly could read well enough the look in his eyes; he was fevering to get a fix off the crack that was Rowan's feeling of rejection.

Rowan after all was Ashton's tacky princess. Right? Forced to stand there, smiling, like a *redneck-hooter-doll* to be abused by everyone, as she stood upon her service throne, she surmised.

One thing she knew for sure.

Her job sucked.

2:00 A.M.
Underneath the Purgatorial Clock of Doom...

Which to her *gloom* was stating the time to be *only* a nasty 2:00 A.M.

Which meant that though it had felt as if she'd been there for an eternity, she still had four hours and fifty-seven minutes more of this to tolerate.

Maybe longer if Doris was late to work, *as she is more often than not.*

Rowan wondered what she had done in a past life that was so bad that she now be demanded to endure such suffering?

This, dead end job Rowan concluded, was the only life fate would allow her if she stayed here - a cruel, thankless existence as the girl with 'the Mother in Law Effect' who only wishes and dreams of the world she wants to see, but is too poor, or too scared, to explore.

The three stoned boys loaded a bunch of snack food in a large pile onto the counter before her. Rowan rang it all up as fast as she could, as there was an awkward silence that hung around the store, and the register gave her the grand total sale price of- "That'll be $64.88." Rowan told them.

The three stooges looked at each other bummed out, and began to haggle over how much each of them owed on the grand total. "Yo, I was just getting the energy drink and the chips, man," said Tiny as he slid his ball cap round his head nervously.

"Hey, I saw you put in these Twizzlers. And the candy bars are not all just mine," said Scott, not wanting to be hustled.

"You are all a bunch of chumps," Tony told his friends, embarrassed that they were haggling when he was trying to look cool. Tony turned towards her: "Yo, Rowan, would you mind if I just pay for my stuff separately?"

"Sounds like the solution..." she told him as she took a deep breath of annoyance, and then proceeded to cancel the large order and to begin processing them separately. As she was doing this, Carl entered the store along with the recipe haggling elderly couple, who were still discussing culinary opinions. He headed directly for the beer cooler, grabbing a six-pack in his arm, and immediately began to pop open one and drink it with the vigor of a man who wants to get drunk quick.

"So Ashley told me that you're not going back to college this year either. What happened?" Tony asked, breaking the silence with an even more awkward question.

"Nope, not this year..." She responded dryly, not caring much to discuss her lack of options with them.

"You're a smart chic. How come you're not going?" Scott inquires.

"Because my parents aren't as rich as yours, that's why, Scotty," she pierced in response.

"Damn, she's feisty tonight." Tony smiled, enjoying that he was getting under her skin. "Rowan, are you still pissed at me or something?"

"That'll be $20.12, Tony..." She holds out her hands for the money.

Tony just leaned in; he gave her a flirting smile. "Why don't you come out with us again?"

"I really don't like your idea of fun." She was not going to play any more games with him, of that she was sure.

"Well I guess that's why you'll be stuck here in this rat hole of a town for the rest of your life, while we go off to college and bright futures. Huh Rowan?" Tony seemed to have an instinct for knowing where to strike a blow.

"Oh damn! Yo, that was a burn and a half, dude." Scott gave him a congratulatory low-five as Tony smoked up the look of hurt upon Rowan's face.

"Fuck off! All of you!" Just like *Grandma Ellian* would have reacted Rowan thought proudly.

Carl Conway quickly approached the counter, his beer in arm, having overheard her. "Did I just hear you tell Tony to fuck off Rowan?" Carl asked in the authoritative voice that always managed to induce her stress level to go off the charts.

"Carl, they are messing with me big-time," Rowan said.

Carl smirked at her; then he looked calmly over at the boys, then back toward Rowan again. *"They're young boys, that's what they do - mess with pretty little th'angs like you."*

"So then why do I not have the right to mess back?"

Carl saw her point and nodded, being a man who enjoyed a good confrontation. "I guess we'll call this one a fair draw then. Alright boys?"

Rowan did *not* think it was fair, at all.

Tony, Scott, and Tiny all nodded in unison and looked at Rowan with smirks and attitude.

"Now, you boys go on and 'git." Carl said, then turned to the boys as they left with their stuffed bags of munchies and pointed out, "And remember boys, you *be good*, and if not, *then you'd better be good at it...*" He proceeded to chuckle - a sinister giggle.

To Rowan's disgust, the three wanna-*be-thug's* began to exit the store, laughing at the coyly suggestive nature of Carl's comment. "Thanks, Conway" said Tony as he pushed through the exit.

Great! Like the 'Dumbtourage' needed any more encouragement toward their already delinquent attitude, than to have a man like Carl egging them toward further debauchery, she thought.

Suddenly remembering something, Carl called out to him before he was gone, "Oh, and Tony, tell your father *I got's that shipment in.* Alright?"

"You got it *Boss*." Tony acknowledged, and then to Rowan's approval they were gone.

"Rowan, you gotta learn to not be such a bitch under pressure," Carl exclaimed to her with a commanding stance, and his arms crossed as he stared at her with the leer of authority and power on his smug face.

"Me?! *They* were the ones who-"

"I don't wanna hear it. Just be nice, no matter what, alright." Carl interrupted her.

Henry and Margaret approached the service counter, having found what they wanted to purchase, still wrangling over recipe preferences.

Rowan had never been so happy to be brought into such drama, and gladly turned toward the distraction.

"No, *I mean it this time,* Margaret," said Henry to her; she replied, "Sure you do."

Henry turned to Rowan and handed her his credit card to pay for the order of items, and inquired: "Why, young lady, you wouldn't happen to have any fine cheeses here, would you?"

Rowan smiled and gave the man a look showing doubt that they have what he wants at Conway's. "All we have is mozzarella cheese sticks in the freezer. And those cheese cracker cup thingies," she told him.

Henry frowned a smile at this, dumbfounded. "What kind of store doesn't carry good cheese out in the countryside?"

Rowan shrugged her shoulders. "Uh, a gas station kind of store that mostly sells smokes and beer, I guess..." wishing they carried good cheese in the dairy cooler; *she would definitely snack on it.*

He smiled another frown, recognizing that she probably was not responsible for choosing the stock of the store. "Yeah I guess. Nice shirt," Henry said to Rowan while not looking in her eyes, but toward her *cheesy chest.*

Of course, she thought, knowing that she couldn't wait until the day she would burn this filthy uniform.

Henry's wife did not like that he was flirting with Rowan and chimed in sorely. "Alright, she said she doesn't have any *cheese* for you Henry, and this *little* girl is busy, so let's go. I still gotta cook the damn thing."

Margaret immediately began herding her husband towards the door, grabbing the bag of groceries as they left. "And all this because you have a craving in the middle of the night, god help me to survive you." Before Henry pushed the door open with a smile, he told his wife, "You keep feeding me your cooking the way you do, you will."

Rowan found it cute that even though they were bickering, she could tell that they really still cared deeply for each other.

As Margaret and Henry exited the store, Murdock approached the counter and rudely tossed the twelve pack of beer onto the counter. It landed with a violent *thump* that rang loud into the tense air. Murdock then pointed to the cigarette shelf behind Rowan and slurred a few words from his very inebriated mouth. "I wan da 'ewporse..."

Of which Rowan could not decipher any meaning. "You want which ones?" She asked timidly.

Murdock was infuriated that Rowan was standing confused, unsure of what he was asking for. "The Newports! The *fucken' EWPORTS!*" Murdock screamed at her, managing this time to be more understandable with his drunken gibberish.

Grabbing the smokes as quickly as she could, she turned back to him with her usual *take no shit* attitude, and pointing to the clock, happily proclaimed to Murdock, "I can sell you the smokes, but gosh-golly-gee it's 2:05 A.M. and we stopped selling alcohol five minutes ago, sir."

"Sucking bish." He grabbed the cigarettes and threw thirty dollars on the counter, then proceeded to take the twelve-pack in his hand anyway, beginning to leave with it.

Rowan looked over to Carl, who had been watching this unfold with a grimy smile upon his face, more watching Rowan's sexy curvature than the interaction, and he didn't even seem to care that Murdock was obviously breaking several laws, most importantly that he was in no condition to be driving at all.

Carl instead took this opportunity to approach Rowan with his yearning eyes and smutty thoughts; he leaned in, making her uncomfortable, as he often did. "What was I just saying to you? Do you even listen to me? The clocks are five minutes fast, and you know that, Rowan. You just sell the man his damned beer!"

Rowan was a little infuriated and shocked that even Carl was being that callous. "Carl, look at him; that guy should clearly not be driving. He could kill someone."

"I didn't hire you to Police my customers, Rowan." Carl's eyes moved from staring at her aggressively and drifted down towards her breasts, again. "I don't see a badge on that shirt; all I see is my sweet name perched on them curves of yours. Honey..."

At this moment, to Rowan's relief, the customer from the fourth car, Vang Cha, entered the store.

Breaking the awkward and hostile sexual advance of her boss from going any further, to Rowan's relief.

Vang immediately got a whiff of the tension happening between her and Carl as the man seemed almost to have her cornered aggressively behind the service counter.

Vang began to approach the counter without any fear in his demeanor, looking to save a damsel in distress.

He found her instantly adorable as he moved closer and got a better look at Rowan.

Vang quickly reassessed as he approached; the cute cashier actually seemed to be doing just fine dealing with the situation on her own, and held a stubborn ground very well against such a larger and obviously out of line man as *Carl Conway.*

Who looked as if he were *Grizzly Adams's* Coke-Head Brother.

Carl Conway turned his hazy gaze toward the approaching Asian fellow, sizing him up with the kind of disdain shown by a man who has prejudices.

But before Carl was able to say whatever stupid thing he was going to say . . .

Suddenly the phone rang.

Carl's eyes darted nervously between staring Vang down and glancing toward the almost antiquated ringing phone in drunken slow motion contemplation.

Carl decided to use this as an excuse to look as if he was busy, and answered the phone. "*Conway's Quikee;* how can I help you?"

Luck being what it was for a man like Carl, he found that on the other end of the line was his wife, who immediately began to chew his ear off about something she was worked up about. Rowan and Vang could both hear the woman furiously screaming at him from where they stood eyeing each other timidly.

Rowan is glad to have the stranger's interjection, and declares to him giddily, "Hi can I help me--*I mean you...*"

The man with wonderful hazel brown eyes, tan skin and delicately settled black hair, said, "What a wave of excitement huh?" nervously trying to break the ice, and hoping he found the right words to do so.

"What?" Rowan's brain was starting to veer into '*mother in law syndrome mode!*'

The man she had never seen before this night smiled warmly at her, and she felt a weakness in her knees that wasn't expected, as he tried to clarify. "All those people showing up all at once so late at night..."

"Oh... Yeah, that's my life, lots of random waves of excitement here at the Quikee..." She laughed nervously.

Another knee melting beam was lobbed from the stranger; Rowan began to feel the flustering of her heart warming her icy mood a bit.

"Sounds like a fun life," he told her.

Rowan almost grunted a laugh of irony, but held it in only to have it spew out as sarcasm, "Yeah... *I love fun.* Who doesn't? Working here's like a carnival of thrills, *yep,*" desperately not wanting him to know that her life *really* was anything but that.

"I like to sometimes go windsailing on the ocean," she added.

The appealing stranger finally posed his need to her. "Do you have any 5W-30?"

Rowan was brain-fart-perplexed by the question, not knowing the answer right offhand. Or even what it was. As she was still transfixed upon his cheerful eyes

"Any what?"

Vang realized the specifics were confusing her. "Do you have any Motor oil?"

Rowan lit up with the answer. "Oh, Of course yes! Motor oil is right this way." She happily left her place at the register and showed Vang down aisle three, to where the oil was stocked.

"It's right here." She waved her hand across the shelf with a smile, like *Vanna White* on that game show.

Rowan watched as Vang grabbed two quarts of 5W-30 and turned back towards her, wasting no time to finally ask her "Is everything alright?"

Rowan was at first confused by the question, then realized he meant was there any trouble between her and the sleazy man behind the counter on the phone, fighting with his wife.

Not sure how to answer such a question without looking absolutely miserable, she found herself saying: "As alright as it ever is..." She attempted to lighten it with another nervous laugh, and then decided it best that she change the subject of conversation to "You're not from around here, huh?"

"*How'd you guess*?" said Vang, trying to make light of the obvious fact that he stuck out like a sore thumb in a mostly white town like Ashton.

Rowan smiled at his sarcasm, it being an art she so much loved. *A man after my heart,* she thought to herself. "It wasn't a hard guess. There are only about twelve people who are from around here. And unfortunately, I know all of them" she playfully asserted to Vang.

He smiled at the absurdity of the statement, and played back. "Twelve people? Really? Just twelve? Are you sure it's not thirteen or fourteen?"

Rowan, enjoying Vang's appreciation of her own personal brand of irony, was very charmed. "Okay, you got me, it's more like several hundred, but they still all feel like the same twelve people none the less. And, I really *do* know most of them..."

"How lucky for everyone," he said.

To Rowan's surprise and joy, she got the feeling that Vang *really* meant it.

"Yeah, well, lucky for me everyone needs gas."

They both enjoyed a delicate moment of silent teasing with their eyes, which was suddenly ruined as-

Carl slammed the phone down, after declaring to his wife, "Listen you troll of a woman! I'm through discussing this with you!" with a rage that Rowan had seen many times before.

Rowan did her best to stay out of Carl's personal business, and never cared to inquire what troubled him. She just did not care. Rowan quickly began to look as if she was still showing the customer where the motor oil was, as Carl turned back towards them.

"I'll see you tomorrow," Carl Conway said, knowing it was time for him to leave.

Rowan just nodded as she turned back towards Vang and the motor oil shelf, as Carl left with his six-pack of beer.

When he was gone, Vang opened up. "When I came in, it just seemed like he was-"

Rowan cut him off with sort of an explanation. "Yes, I know. My boss is kind of a scumbag. But I'm fine; really, I know how to handle him. You know I'm a Lion-Tamer after all..."

"A Lion-Tamer; Really? Well - that's marvelous. I'm sure that skill comes in handy in Moose territory." And like most men, of course, had to comment about the insignia on her chest. But, she liked the way he coyly snuck it in to her setup, so found it endearing instead of the usual disgust.

"My name's Vang by the way." He said as they shared another nervous and flirtatious smile; unsure if she was offended by his moose comment.

She made it quickly apparent that she was not bothered at all, "Nice to meet you, Vang. My name's Rowan." She wondered what culture his name derived from.

"So why don't you find another job if your boss is like that, Rowan?"

"You're really suggesting there is actually another job available in this place called *Nowhere?*" she was quick to point out.

"Yeah, you know... If you're not finding what you want here? Then why not look elsewhere?"

"What I want and what I can do are not always in agreement."

"So what's stopping you?" Vang inquired.

"Money. Lack of a car... Are just a few of the things stopping me."

"Yeah, I understand that. Maybe we could win one of these lottery tickets? And then you could quit this job?" as he pointed to one of the scratch-off lottery tickets. "How about that one?" Vang's finger had selected the One Dollar Lotto ticket with a large bunny rabbit holding up a bunch of carrots, and each of the nine golden carrots was a possible scratch off winner; it was called *9 karats of luck!*

Rowan, amused, grabbed the scratch-off ticket while retrieving a dollar from her pocket; and quickly transacted the sale. She then leaned in, took a penny from the loose change tray on the counter, and began scratching.

"How much do you think we're gonna win?" Vang inquired.

"Nothing. Nobody ever wins here; this place is like cursed or something." She scoffed as she scratched away.

Only to reveal a winning ticket ironically.

Rowan looked to double check, and sure enough, she had won a whole two dollars!

Seeing that she was a winner, Vang gave Rowan a huge grin to her and joyously stated, "Well, it looks like we just changed that. She's a winner."

"Amazing, two dollars! Wahoo, where will we fly?" she declares, thick with irony.

Vang laughed at her cynical attempt at a joke. "You still doubled your money; you have to admit it's statistically impressive."

"Let's do two more," she said, wanting to find any excuse to keep the charming man in her presence.

Vang smirked at her as he lifted an eyebrow. "Are you sure you don't wanna quit while you're ahead?

"Which ones should I play this time?" She asked him.

"You pick them this time," he responded, not wanting to command her choices.

"But you're my lucky charm," she assured him.

"Your lucky charm, huh?" Vang liked that Rowan thought he was her lucky charm, and so he chose two more scratch off tickets, which she immediately ripped away from the pack, cashing in the $2 winner to pay for them. Rowan then clenched the penny between her thumb and index finger tightly, and begins to scratch away at the tickets with a sense of hope and possibility jumping in her heart; *maybe just maybe these tickets could change everythin-*

Nope... The tickets were losers.

"I won -- Nothing!" She said with a glee as if she'd actually won the Publishers Clearing House.

"Oh well, maybe next time." Vang consoled her loss.

"Yeah, *maybe*. Life is filled with maybes. Right? *And,* maybe my boss will wake up tomorrow, stop being a skuzz-ball, and give me a raise. Oh, and *maybe* tomorrow the world will stop fighting all those wars, or do something about global warming," Rowan listlessly added as a tangent, then realized that perhaps she came off as too bleak.

"Hey, you never know; it really could happen," Vang said hopefully.

"Yeah, it could, and the sky will rain Twinkies, too..." she said with a flirting charm and smirk trying to lesson the gloom of her speech.

"Hey, I warned you to walk away while you were ahead," Vang darted back.

"Well, next time I'll know to take your advice," she admitted to Vang, trying to find another excuse to keep talking to him, as she wasn't wealthy enough to keep losing money playing the lotto.

"So what brings you to Ashton?" she decided was a good way of easing the conversation forward.

"I'm kind of on a journey, taking the long way home." Vang decided this was the best way of describing his spiritual *'soul calling'* to her at the moment.

"Wow, a journey, huh?" she inquired with her best effort to appear alluring in her voice and body language, wanting to talk with him all night long. "So, what's the difference between journeying and regular traveling?"

"Spiritual Intention," Vang made clear.

"What, like god leading the way and all?" Wondering now if he is actually one of those Latter Day Saints missionary converts, or a Jehovah's Witness.

"Not exactly." Vang always had a difficult time trying to explain his families' foreign religious practices and belief to Americans, though he was always trying. "It's more like connecting with family and friends and finding inner strengths and such..."

"Yeah, well I don't know about yours, but you'd have to have a lot of inner strength to connect with my family," she admitted self-deprecatingly.

"Yeah I hear you... And bosses too. Right?"

"Right," she said, gazing into his thoughtful eyes, Rowan wished upon the lightning flashing in the sky outside, secretly at that moment, she desired that this man would *'journey' into her life,* for more than just some lubricant for his engine, and fuel for his car.

But she knew that the green machine outside waiting for its owner, would soon be headed forever away from her, carrying the man of her dreams with it.

It happened to her all the time, a man would enter, flirt with her, then after a little fun midnight chitchat, the beautiful patrons always, all of them, ended up saying the same bittersweet thing: *'Well, thanks. It was nice meeting you... goodbye...'* And then they would all drive out of her life, and just keep moving along, never to return.

Why would they?

There was no reason ever to come back to Ashton, she thought disappointingly.

"Well, it was nice meeting you Rowan. Thanks..." said Vang as expected to Rowan's disapproval...

"Nice meeting you too. Sir Vang," she said to him as he grabbed the motor oil he had bought, readying his exit.

"It's Vang Cha, actually," he informed her with a deep comfort in his vocal tone.

"That's a beautiful name; what ethnicity is it from?" Her words fluttered from her mouth like doves rising towards the clouds.

"Hmong."

"Mung? Like the Bean?" She was immediately embarrassed that she had just callously *equated his entire racial existence to a freak'in bean?!*

Rowan began to think of something witty to say that would save her from looking completely like a dumb redneck, but before she could, to her delight, she saw that Vang found humor in it.

He chuckled at her honest attempt to say the word, knowing quite well that language is like anything else, like riding a bike or such; you never get it right the first time round.

"I get that a lot; it's hilarious. It's pronounced *'hmô ng',*" he said more slowly for her, to clarify its pronunciation, hoping that she doesn't find the way he did it condescending.

She didn't; she actually appreciated his taking the time to help her learn, as she attempted another honestly humble go at saying it right. "*Mhông?*" she said.

"Almost there this time." Excited that she was seriously attentive, he at that moment wished he met more American women like her; she was authentically interested in him, it appeared.

"Hmô ng," he tried one more time, enjoying her company.

"Hmô ng," she said, getting it right this time.

Vang congratulated her. "That's really good, third time's the charm, *eh*?"

Rowan is pleased she got it right as she takes note of his Canadian use of the word: *eh.* "Canadian, huh? I *love* Canada."

"Oh yeah, you've been there?" he asked, wanting to know more about her.

"Yeah, I've been up to Montreal several times over the past few years," fondly recalling in her mind the few fun nights she spent as a drunken tourist with her friends - before they had all left for college - when she had just turned eighteen several years before, and could legally drink up there. "Where in Canada are you from?"

"I'm not; I'm actually American. But I grew up in Michigan, near Canada."

"Oh so they speak Canadian in Michigan, then?" They both smirked at the joke; Rowan wondered what life on the great lakes would be like. Just like living on the ocean, except with smaller waves, and less smelly, she theorized. "That's near Toronto, right?" She said.

"Yeah, but my parents immigrated from Vietnam before I was born, and they had learned how to speak English from a Canadian, so the *eh's,* kind of became a part of my family's speech patterns. Funny, *eh*?"

"So you're Vietnamese?" She then jokingly mimicked an "*eh?*"

It was complicated to answer that question precisely, and Vang didn't want to bore her with the intricate details of the ethnic nuances of *South*

East Asia, so he just responded: "Not exactly; but sort of."

"That's wild." Being a curious person, she realized she needed to *Wikipedia* this conversation to learn more about the Hmong culture.

She then politely solicited more chitchat, without looking too anxious, "So why are you *'journeying'* through a place like Ashton? *That is;* if you don't mind me asking?"

"I go to school in Boston and I'm on my way back home to a big family reunion, which happens every year around this time," Vang informed her to her heart's dismay.

"That's awesome..." *Not really.* It meant that the usual *'goodbye forever'* was on its way, and that she would never be able to get to know him better; she would just be that girl who could say a word in his language right, once upon a time, and whose name he'd soon forget.

Vang looked up at the clock on the wall to see that the time was 2:14 a.m.

Rowan scornfully peered toward the forsaken timepiece, which so suddenly had chosen to move too fast *now,* as the enjoyable moment was going to be fleeting away from her, at the average road speed of a *Ford Gran Torino.*

Vang was now at the moment of his inevitable departure.

She had a strange thought: *what if her life was actually just some sort of twisted episode of 'The Twilight Zone'?*

'What if her whole life was just one constant parade of lovely men that she couldn't ever touch?' Rowan's inner doubt spoke to her quietly.

'*What if she never got to love anyone - ever again?*

Yeah, that was Ashton; *a twisted purgatory placed between heaven and hell, that her life would forever exist in!?*'

"Well, maybe we'll meet again." The words were like pinpricks of agony to Rowan's ears.

Wherever *Ashton really was* did not matter to Rowan, because right now to her, it was much closer to *Hell* than anything else.

Of that, she was sure...

"Yeah, that'd be great..." she said; then her crying inner redneck-clown-princess added mournfully, *Yeah, like that'll happen...* But she decided to inform Vang before he had left the store, just in case it is possible: "I'm here, anytime on the night shift 6 days a week. Except on Sundays... " Then thoughtfully added, "I hope you enjoy your family gathering."

"Alright, thanks. I'm sure I will." He said in response, then added, "I hope you enjoy the rest of your night"

"I'll try..." She said. But would not. "Bye..."

"Goodbye. And hey- remember, you never know what the future holds for you." Vang said, and respectfully nodded as he exited the store, giving her the most wonderful smile as he went.

The store was lonely once again, just like her life felt, and unfortunately Rowan believed she knew all to well what future lay in wait for her at that moment. She watched as Vang looked back at her through the store window and smiled at her one last time, the gusting wind splashing his hair, as he got into his faded Ford Torino.

She smiled back, and even waved at him, as his car pulled away. When he was gone she stopped waving her hand giddily and exhaled a gasp of aggravation as she grabbed the half drank beer that Carl Conway had left behind on the counter and angrily tossed it in the trash.

"Way to go Rowan. First cute guy to walk in here in a thousand years, and you show him how sophisticated you are..." she mocked herself out loud to a lonesome store, waving another good-bye to no one, thinking to herself that she must have looked ridiculous. "*Goodbye*... I waved!? Like a fucking cheerleader, I'm such a dork..."

She then looked out the window at the empty parking lot. '*I'll never see him again.*' Rowan's mind synchronized with the bolts of lightning illuminating the sky over Ashton, and the thought of *thunder* followed... Rumbling in both the heavens above and the hell within.

2:16 A.M.

Rowan's eyes compulsively were drawn toward looking up at Ashton's dreary version of Big Ben once again to be tormented further, when suddenly, *the lights went out.*

All power ceased in the entire store.

Everything was dead quiet.

"*Come on*, really!" Rowan shouted to the ceiling, and God or whatever sick force of nature ruled over her world, as she exited the store and looked around to try to figure out what was happening.

She noticed the streetlights were still working; yet the store was dark and powerless. All was eerily quiet, that is until a boom of thunder drum rolled across the sky to add to the mood.

Finding this odd - and clearly above her pay grade as a problem - Rowan pulled her cell phone from her pocket, and prepared to call Carl, but before she could, a woman's voice crept up from behind her and said: *"Just my luck! The power's out..."*

Rowan was instantly startled, and turned around to find a woman in her late twenties or early thirties, dressed well in a very urban high maintenance kind of way. She had lots of expensive looking jewelry ornamenting her body and was holding a small purse while elegantly trying to smoke a cigarette.

"Oh my god, you scared me..." she said, relieved that the woman was not some creepy dude, or worse, Bigfoot or whatnot.

"Sorry, sugar, didn't mean to sneak up on you like that." Seeing Rowan was still spooked a little by her sudden intrusion, she went to try and break the ice, "My name's Cindy, by the way; nice to meet yah."

"My name's Rowan," not waiting for her to ask.

"The freak'in powers out?! ... What a fuckin' night, I'll tell yah *girl!*" The woman then proceeded to exclaim a very huffy and sassy *"Ahhhhhhh!"*

Rowan couldn't have said it better herself, *"Yep...* I never get the easy nights; this place is just *too damned weird and crazy..."* Rowan huffed grudgingly to her, then confided. "My life sucks!"

"I know what you mean girl. B'cause that's exactly what I just told my man... MmmHmm." Then added, "Shit." She nodded the lit and almost entirely smoked cigarette in her hand towards Rowan. "This is *my last one.*" Immediately the city slick woman proposed: "You wouldn't mind if I just gave you an *Andrew Jackson* for a couple of packs of smokes*;* and then you can just keep the change?" She proceeded to wink at Rowan with the warm smile of a girl who knows how to get what she wants.

Rowan returned the warmness, liking the way the woman carried herself, "Sure. Why not? But first I gotta tell my boss about our little problem." Rowan began preparing to dial Carl's number, as duty called first.

The woman pulled out a hundred dollar bill from her purse quickly. "How about I give you a G-Spot? That is if you're willing to get it for me right *now,* before you make the phone call? Huh? I'm kind of a nicotine fiend, and this's been one hell of a night, sugar. I'd love you *forever..."*

Rowan without a pause pocketed the phone for

the moment and re-entered the store to get the woman a pack of smokes; not at all did the thought even cross her mind to pass up such an opportunity.

"No problem. Which kinds do you smoke?"

The woman followed along. "Got anything Natural, or Organic? You know, without all them chemicals and such?"

"Why yes we do. Regular, milds, or lights?"

"Oh you're an angel. I'll have the Lights please."

Rowan hands Cindy two packs of her choice, but she wants to be sure the lady isn't just yanking her chain. "You're really going to give me a hundred for a couple packs of smokes?"

The city girl looked at her and shined the saying: *"A girls gotta have what she's gotta have"* from her glossed cherry red lips. "And you look like you could use it." She then ripped the pack of fresh cigarettes open skillfully, and popped one stick out and lit it in almost one fluid motion.

Rowan was astonished by the casual attitude of the woman paying a hundred dollars for a pack of smokes, but was not willing to complain about receiving the largest tip of her life for just one minute of easy work. *This is a Vegas kind of Gal; a 'High Roller'* was Rowan's first impression of Cindy.

"Thanks." Rowan said, as she led Cindy back towards the stores exit, and to the parking lot, where her phone's reception was ideal, on top of the fact that it was illegal to be smoking inside a public establishment in their state.

Cindy, who followed Rowan back outside and into the stormy weather, appeared to have Goosebumps and was certainly well under dressed for the chilly weather, approaching them fast from the Atlantic Ocean.

"*B'sides,* my boyfriend's been a little bit of a jerk tonight, so *that's* not a very big deal to me at the moment; *I'm just relieved to get my Nic-Fix.*" said Cindy. She then took an extended and ponderous drag from the smoke in her right hand, which Rowan could see in the hue from the street lamps had fingernails that were hand painted with gold Japanese writing. "*Know what I mean?*" The woman then added another jittery smile, and to boot her overpowering suave attitude, she added a very relieved "MMhhmm..." with her exhale.

"Not really. I don't smoke... But I do crave Snickers bars a lot. So I guess perhaps I have *Snick-fits*?" Rowan admitted to her new-charmed friend.

Cindy laughed. "I know, *fucking sugar*! Makes y'ah fat and it's *fuckin'* more addictive than heroin and nicotine, and it's everywhere and in everything! Or so they say... Man, it's getting *chilly,* and quick," the very out of place woman said, folding her arms across her chest, shivering.

Rowan decided that she could offer this woman her extra coat in the back room to keep her warm, and was about to do so, when –

Suddenly a black Subaru Outback came screeching into the stores parking lot at around a very dangerous thirty or so miles per hour, and then came to an abrupt skidding halt near the front door of the store, just about ten feet from where they stood. Out of it, a man excitably pounced, disturbingly much worked up about something.

The Latino man in his late thirties was also

urbanely dressed, with tattoos showing on his exposed arms, a black dyed wife-beater shirt and sporting a well trimmed goatee along with the ever urbanized fashion cliché of a slanted ball cap with the word *"ASYLUM"* written on it.

"Come on, Cindy, we gotta go *now!*" He declared loudly. The man almost seemed to be hysterical with a brooding intensity, and proceeded to run directly up to Cindy and excitably, but gently, grabbed her left hand and began to pull her towards the car.

Cindy pushed the very gruff boyfriend away with the attitude of a woman scorned. "I am not going anywhere with you. We're through. You've been'ah complete *asshole* this whole evening *Jackson!*" and puffs a final *"So you can just buzz off!" Followed* by a very serious finger snap in his face that meant she was on the warpath with him.

Jackson was impatient. "I could *give a fuck* about earlier. Right now we are in danger! We don't have time to do this Cindy. We have to get out of here *right now!*"

Rowan heard the Emergency Broadcast System's very distinct pitching sound blaring from the ambient radio, and instead of being followed by the usual *'this is a test'* chatter – instead - news began streaming on the stereo; it was talking about some *"Tsunami warning"* that had been declared.

The man speaking on the radio sounded as if he were a British Broadcaster speaking a very important warning from a BBC radio station to everyone *"in the coastal regions of the northeastern parts of the United States and Canada on the Atlantic Ocean."* The news jockey very melodramatically said with an officiating voice of great magnitude, *"Evacuation protocols for all people living within these areas have been issued, and everyone living within these coastal regions is advised to immediately evacuate to higher ground."*

Rowan started to have an eerie shiver creep into her mind, as she began to feel the *Twilight Zone* slipping into her reality.

"Ain't gonna play me no more, I tell you that; boy... You can't sugar talk y'er way out of this one, sorry."

"Listen to me damn'it! *There's a giant Tsunami wave headed straight for us as we speak; I don't know how much time we have left.* So, we must go *now!* Okay?"

Cindy and Rowan both: "What!?"

And Rowan, stunned, added "Oh my god," as the realization set in that almost everyone she knew and loved was at this very moment sleeping, and in no way able to evacuate.

Cindy threw her arms up in the air. "Go where? Huh Jackson? We're in the middle of *nowhere!"* pointing out the obvious fact that that the area is on the coast and pretty darn flat.

"I don't know - to higher ground, as fast as possible *is where,"* he said, and then without skipping a beat he shouted, "So get in the *fucking car* and let's go! Alright?!"

"You are such a jackass. I can't believe you said that about me earlier!" as if she hadn't even heard a word he had said, only ready to retort with her rehearsed rant. It didn't seem to matter to her that a major catastrophe was unfolding outside her high maintenance existence.

Rowan found this a little disturbing, and so did Jackson.

"Have you heard a word I've just said? Listen, listen to me!" Jackson grabbed both her arms with his hands and shook her as he went eye to eye with her, then said sternly, "There is a giant fucking Tsunami headed our way, *right now,* and we gotta go, *right now.* Get it sweetness?"

Rowan admired how calm he seemed, as the tension of the moment's epiphany began to wobble her like seasickness. She could feel her tumultuous stomach wanting to hurl the snickers break up suddenly, but she managed to hold it back, as she looked up at them and said: *"Perkins' Pier!"*

"What?" asks Cindy.

"That's the highest point closest to here. If I remember my grandma's geography lessons correctly, that is. It's, I believe, uhm about five hundred feet above sea level. It's this local park up this road on these cliffs overlooking the ocean. It's, you know, *'the make out place'...*" She twitched a sigh from her exasperated self, and notified them that "It's also only a ten minute drive from here, as well."

Rowan and Cindy both turned to the car and finally gave an attentive listen to what the radio broadcaster was saying on the stereo. *"The reports are coming in now from Nova Scotia; there have been terrible earthquake tremors all throughout the region along its southern coastlines-"* Suddenly the feed was interrupted by the sounds of the official alert warning again. Rowan and Cindy had heard enough to realize that what he said was true; it was time to exodus quickly...

"Yep, Yep, Let's get moving," Cindy agreed finally. She skipped, rushed, towards the shotgun seat of Jackson's car, muttering to herself while fanning her face with her purse, very hot and bothered. "Oh lordy-lordy...." Jackson too wasted no time; he took the helm of the vehicle and prepared to leave.

Rowan, a little distressed, watched as Cindy and Jackson began, hurriedly, to get into the Subaru to leave. Realizing she had no car, she yelled out to them before they could leave, *"Hey!"*

Cindy and Jackson paused in their excitement, and both turned their heads to peer over at her.

"You're not just gonna leave me here? I don't have a car..."

Cindy jolted to action and unlocked the rear passenger door, "Get in sugar."

Rowan was about to jump into the car, but stopped short, she then turned and ran over, quickly locking the store's door with a key from her pocket. Rowan immediately hundred yard dashed back towards Jackson's car and shot herself into the back seat, whipping the door closed behind her, as Cindy, fastening her seat belt, warned her: "And buckle up, Sugar; my boy Jackson here is a wild driver..."

Jackson turned to Cindy, offended by the statement. "Hey, I am not." As he floored the car's gas pedal, they were all thrust back into their seats to the sound of now screeching tires.

Jackson's car sped forward from the gas station as fast as it could.

"Where's this pumpkin peer? Am I going in the right direction?" Jackson asked as he scoped Rowan's eyes through the rearview mirror.

"Uhm... Perkins Pier, and yeah." Rowan was trying to gather her bearings. "Just go straight for a while." The stress was building quickly in her mind, body, and heart. Thoughts raced between her loved ones and the directions to the destination of safety. Rowan had an assessment that this was not the kind of 'life change' she'd been hoping for.

As Jackson programmed into his GPS the name of the place they were headed, down the road, on the other side of the divider, sparkled upon them all some headlights from an approaching vehicle. And as they passed the car, Jackson flashed his high beams on and then immediately turned them dim again. The passing vehicle repeated this action as well, and just kept going.

Rowan got a glimpse of Oscar's face as the other car passed by; it was the face of an angry man, his brow heavy with menace.

Rowan wondered if he was also listening to the radio and freaking out. She was sad she had no way to tell the man he was headed the wrong way.

The three of them just raced away into the stormy night, eerily, as if the storm itself was in unison with the sudden Armageddon upon them all, flashing more lightning over them, and laughing a thunderous chorus of ominous drum rolls from the East.

Rowan felt a sinking feeling of how truly fleeting life really is, as the British announcer on the radio spoke onward, *"A Tsunami warning is in effect for all the eastern coasts of Canada, and the United States."*

Rowan began to feel panic overtake her. *"Which seems to have been caused by a massive landslide off the coast of the island nation Cape Verde and is believed to have been triggered by a large volcanic explosion deep in the ocean on the tectonic plate of the region. Cape Verde is in the archipelagos island nation just off the cast of Africa near-"*

Jackson pressed the eject button on his CD console; the stereo went quiet, as a disc was ejected from the car's console. He then replaced the CD with one that he had tucked in his car's visor.

A very loud crackled voice began to sing, as he played melancholy mood music. They headed down the dark country road, fast.

"Don't you want to keep the news on?" Rowan asked Jackson; unsure why under the circumstances he just turned off their information feed.

"We've been warned; I don't need to hear it a thousand times over," he said, content to no longer be stressed out by it.

Rowan looked through the windshield to see a white church steeple flashing in the sudden spark of lightning darting in the stormy sky ahead of them. She realized where they were and declared, while pointing: "Turn left up at the next road!"

Jackson was unsure about the advice, as his GPS was telling him to go straight, still. "I don't know? That's not what my tech is telling me."

"Well your tech is wrong. Both these roads go there; the next left onto Flanders is a quicker shortcut; trust me..."

"Just listen to her; she works at the fuckin' gas station, for god's sake," Cindy barks at him, her patience still razor thin with him.

"Alright, fine," Jackson relented, and he did as she said, taking the left turn onto Flanders Road and heading up a long and winding road, deeper into the darkness of the quiet country night, with electricity still dashing in the storm clouds in the distant sky on the horizon, illuminating the pine tree rimmed road ahead of them. Rowan decided it was time to send *'shout outs'* to as many family and friends as possible.

Her heart swelled as the rush of people listed off in her mind like a barrage of snapshots. Her Mom and Dad.

Her Aunt Shelly, Her cousins Dahlia and Maria, Joseph and Tyson.

And Alice, Brad, Angela, Moe, Allen, Tim, Chris!

Then there were also Brian, Sharon, Dennis, Evan, Sarah, Kahlil, Bob, and Celia....

Her entire town!

The entire fucking east coast!...

Hell, if she had time, even Carl deserved a call, she figured.

Motivation seized her at this moment as her neurons began to get over the initial shock of the events thrust upon them all so suddenly. Rowan took her phone from her jean pockets, and began to scroll down to her parents' number in her contacts list.

Cindy noticed Rowan about to make a phone call and nudged Jackson with her knee; he was taken from his calm enjoyment of the music as he looked over to her and watched her eyes dart toward Rowan in the back seat.

He glared through the rear view mirror at what was happening and immediately jumped his foot on the brakes urgently, and the station wagon skidded along the road sideways.

Rowan's cell phone was thrust from her hands, went flying into the front of the vehicle, and was lost in the darkness of the car's interior, as they were all jolted suddenly forward. Seatbelts snagged them, and they whiplashed backward as the car's brakes locked to a sudden stop.

Cindy began to yap Jackson's Ear off about it. "You're seriously never going to drive me anywhere ever again."

"Sorry, I thought I saw a Dog in the road," he said in defense to her contempt for his actions.

Jackson immediately floored the gas pedal again.

"See, I told you he was a horrible driver," Cindy said, turning back towards Rowan with a flummoxed smirk.

"Where's my phone? I have to call my parents and warn them," Rowan declared with a terrified undertone in her voice, not at all sure how Cindy was capable of finding a smile at a time such as this. She began to search for her phone, leaning down and reaching her arms underneath the car seats, desperately trying to see if she could find it.

"I need to find my phone."

Jackson turned to Cindy. "Help her *find the damned phone...*"

Cindy did as asked, and leaned down to help look for the phone. She reached her arms about while she watched Rowan ducking low in the back seats, looking, still only to come up empty. "We'll find it when we stop soon. Okay?" Cindy tried to console her, to no avail.

"That might be too late. I have to call them!" Rowan responded distractedly, still trying to find the mysteriously missing phone.

Cindy appeased her and continued to help Rowan look for the phone.

Still nothing.

Rowan was confused as to where it could have

gone, as she still frantically searched for it, aware that time right now was precious; time was fleeting away, plunging, rushing towards them at the speed of a Tsunami, which Rowan at this moment was remembering travel at speeds equal to modern jetliners.

This thought added a sense of terror to her already frenzied search for her phone.

"Do either of you have a phone I can use?" Rowan petitioned suddenly, fed up.

She was now worried that she might have trouble remembering everyone's phone numbers off the top of her head.

"Naw, sorry, our phones were left at the motel," Jackson apologetically informed her, as he continued to gun the Subaru Outback along the road on a mission to get to high ground.

"This can't be happening..." Rowan began to freak out. "Everyone's going to die... *My- god...*"

Jackson was obviously unsettled by Rowan's tumultuous behavior in the back seat of his car as he was driving, and turned to Cindy, growling at her: "Can you get her to chill out?!

Rowan leaned into the car's middle divider between the two front seats, having heard his remark, and talked as loud as she could, trying to compete with the blaring music.

"Can you turn that music down?! Maybe it'll help me *chill out if I could hear myself think!*" she bit back.

Jackson began to feel his tension rise; being yelled at in the ear was a pet peeve that put him in foul moods.

But he just bit his tongue and *'sucked it up.'* Doing as Rowan asked, he softened his stereo, so she could be heard.

He was a good soldier; a cool headed soldier, he told himself as he drove onward towards the cliffs, trying not to lose it.

Cindy turned to her apologetically. "We'll find it; just relax."

"Relax?! We need to *do something* to help everyone! My family *is going to die*! I *need* to find my Phone. We need to warn everyone about the Tsunami."

"But what can we do? We have *no time* to help anyone dear..."

"Of course there's time, we have too - I mean like, at least we could honk our horn and scream Tsunami or something, *anything!*"

Deaf ears were all her words fell on.

Rowan tried to reason with them, "Most people around here are sleeping right now."

But they seemed to be unbendable, curiously unconcerned about anyone else but themselves, as Jackson continued to speed as fast as his car would take them, saying to her, "There's no time for that; we gotta save *ourselves*..."

Rowan watched as they approached a familiar road marker, a giant Native American carved wooden bear totem lit up with two spotlights, and she noticed Vang's *Ford Torino* parked along the side of the road underneath it.

Suddenly, her heart was encompassed with dread.

"Stop!" Rowan pleaded with them, wanting to warn Vang Cha that he was in peril. "I know him; we need to warn him! We need to warn everyone!"

"There's no time!" Jackson said, a little wound up, as his fists clenched the wheel at ten and two o'clock in his attempt to focus on getting them to higher ground as soon as possible, and he just kept on driving away from the giant wooden statue of a Bear, under which was parked her new friend Vang.

Rowan oddly was struck with the realization that the man singing on the radio was *Leonard Cohen*, and he was profoundly singing one of her favorite old songs. She could only watch as they passed Vang by, and was maddened; the sad thought that she had no power to stop any of this pounded her like a hammer to the chest.

She really was helpless.

Rowan, unable to save him, could only hope that Vang Cha would journey to safety. She hoped for it *deeply* as she saw his car fade away into the distance. It slapped her in the face, the thought that she *might never see any of them ever again...*

She thought feverishly about what could be done in the moment, but was frozen in agony, unable to find a way to help him, or anyone.

She was powerless to stop the tides of time and circumstance.

Real life isn't like the movies; there were no real heroes, no angels that swooped in to protect you when things got bad. *That's why it's called fiction*, she thought scornfully.

There was no loving god.

No *superwoman.*

No Batman. She couldn't just fly to the rescue and save the day...

That's not the way things worked on planet earth, especially in a place like Ashton.

Chaos was all there was to the universe; now that was a truth Rowan feared she was hard pressed to refute.

Tears began to flood from Rowan's emotionally welled eyes, as she looked through the rear window of the hatchback vehicle. Only to watch as everything outside sped away from her.

Probably forever...

Rowan was petrified.

The road they were driving upon suddenly broke out onto the edge of a massive cliff, and the car curved along a rocky shelf - which overlooked the stormy Atlantic Ocean to the East.

In the distance, several hundred feet below them, Rowan watched the lighthouse weather the angry seas, its ship beacon rhythmically pulsing steadily in the lightning strobe darkness, as she was charioted away, as *Leonard* sang a mournful song on the stereo, ever so sweetly as they fled into the turbulent night...

Rowan oddly had one thing on her mind:

What time is it?..

Several Minutes Previously: 2:27 A.M.

He had chosen the spot to get his bearings for the simple fact that he wanted a picture of the giant *Native American totem poll* of a bear standing on top of a tortoise; upon its shoulders stood a hawk - whose eyes were gazing toward the place where the sun rose in the fiery east.

His mission having been accomplished, Vang Cha was then in the process of looking at his ragged and outdated *Road Atlas* trying to find a great place to sit and eat a snack from his cooler while watching the coming storm roll in off the ocean; when he looked up, he watched as Jackson's Subaru raced by.

He was shocked, noticing that Rowan was in the back seat of the car, looking quite frantic and alarmed. Vang found it very odd, remembering that she told him her schedule, and then concern shuffled in as he recalled the sketchy scene he had walked into earlier at the store she worked at.

Vang Cha's chivalry set in immediately.

As was his nature, he was not going to turn the other way and ignore a person in need - especially one as cute and charming as Rowan.

He put his Atlas down, geared his car forward, and began to follow them.

Though he was young, having grown up in some rough parts of Minnesota with three sisters, he had long been schooled in the carnal dangers of the world around him.

Vang needed to know if she was okay, and was unconcerned at the time of the dangers that can come with curiosity.

2:33 A.M.

Jackson parked the car near some trees in the park called Perkins Pier, which had stone monuments and picnic tables, with a lookout over the grand ocean expanse before them, over which the rain clouds were brewing lightning and thunder for them all to imbibe soon enough.

The wind picked up as Jackson, Cindy and Rowan exited the car to look out over the view.

Rowan immediately looked out over the dark ocean, looking for signs of the impending Tsunami, but it was too dark to tell what was happening; the only thing she could see was lightning flashing in the storm clouds over the ocean and the lighthouse's skipping heartbeat.

Rowan turned back to the car to look for the phone one more time, knowing that it *must* be there somewhere. She opened the front passenger side door and dove down to the rug, her mission to find the phone more than an obsession right now; it was a necessity that she find it, a matter of life and death.

Jackson was annoyed that she was rifling through his car so vigorously. As Cindy gave him a smile and caressed his hair charmingly, giving him a wink, she whispered in his ear so that Rowan could not overhear, "It's all right; I got it." Jackson watched as she coyly, without Rowan seeing, flashed the missing cell phone from her pocket, so that Jackson could see she had it. Jackson was relieved.

Coming up empty from searching the car again, Rowan began to pace the parking lot, wondering how it just vaporized into thin air.

"Where the hell did it go? How can it have just vanished like that?"

"Sorry you can't find your phone, Sweetie," Cindy said, turning to soothe Rowan's hyper-distressed mood. "I'm sure everything will be fine; you just watch."

Rowan was worried for her family, and her fear was in a fever stage now, as she paced, trying to think of anything that could be done to save her loved ones. "What can we do? My family is down there sleeping right at sea level!"

Jackson looked to her with an icy shuffle in his stance. "There is nothing we can do except wait, and hope all turns out well... This is an act of God..."

Rowan does not know what to say to that.

"It probably won't be more than a little wave once it hits here; I'm sure everything is gonna be okay," said Cindy, worried at how Rowan is taking all this excitement.

Rowan is trying to calm herself down now, by taking deeper breathes and pacing less. "You're right... I mean how bad could it be? Positive thinking, you're right; we need to hope everything will be fine." Rowan tries to agree with her, though her voice still crackles with doubt at the idea.

"You know, I once was in a store during an armed robbery; and I remember being scared as hell..." Cindy tells her.

"Really?" Rowan wasn't very interested in stories right now.

Cindy didn't care and just kept talking. "I prayed for a guardian angel to protect me... And you know what? God answered my prayers, and everything turned out alright..."

Rowan sat down on a rock and looked out over the dark horizon once more, fearful still, but not as frantic. She took a deep breath to try and regain her bearings.

Cindy, happy to see she was relaxing a little, decided it was a good time to try and talk about happier things and said: "So, what are your plans? You know; for the rest of your life?"

Rowan found the non sequitur out of place, yet realized she was just trying to help take her mind off the worry, and played into the conversation changer. "I'm still trying to figure that out..." then sadly pondered aloud to them both, "But what life will I have left after the Tsunami hits?.."

"How old are you?"

Cindy felt her pain and tried to calm her worry the best she could.

"Twenty-one."

"Let me share with you something I wish I had known at twenty-one but have only started to understand about life just recently," Cindy sternly said.

Rowan, with her head slung low and defeated, gave in to Cindy's need to try and pep talk her out of panic attack. "Oh yeah what's that?"

"That we have no control over what goes on in the world; we only have control over how we *face* those challenges. You need to be strong, and hopeful, and you'll see everything can turn out well."

Cindy got a whiff from Rowan's dismayed look that she may be layering it on a little thick. "Oh I sound too preachy. I'm sorry..." She decided she needed a cigarette and began to rustle through her purse for the pack.

"No, it was beautiful... You're right. I need to be strong. Think positive thoughts..." Rowan submitted to her, looking up toward the horizon to see that the storm was almost upon them now.

"So, what are your dreams? What are your passions? What makes you horny?" Cindy teased her giddily as she lit the smoke. They both chuckled and shared an ironic smile. Rowan: "I don't know... The sky... I guess you could say I'm passionate about that."

Cindy smiled, sitting and joining Rowan on the rock, next to her in a comforting way.

"And the stars... The planets, anything really that has to do with the wonder and amazement of what's out there in the sky." Rowan and Cindy both looked out at the storm brewing, watching lightning flashing across storm clouds.

As if to agree with Rowan's statement: "Yeah. I've always loved that stuff too," said Cindy.

Jackson, rolling his eyes decided it was time for some refreshment and grabbed three beers from the car. Without delay, he cracked one open and began chugging. After taking a gulp that entirely emptied the can, he tipped it back away from his lips and looked around; attentively, something was bothering him so he scanned the area like a predator, and then checked his watch nervously to see that the time was 2:45 A.M.

Jackson's did not like feeling exposed, and right now, that was the situation. As he cracked open another beer, and began to down it as quick as the previous one, his bladder began to swell towards the demand to relieve itself, and he began searching for a place to urinate.

* *21 MINUTES PREVIOUSLY*
2:24 A.M.

Oscar had jumped off his first bridge when he had been nine years old. His desire to leap one was born when his mother one day had heatedly asked him while livid at some tiny misbehaving, *'what?! Are you going to jump off a bridge too if all your friends were doing it?!'*

Well, unfortunately, to his mother's fright, and being a *'chip off the old block'* of his dad, he thought that *actually, yes - he would go jumping off bridges.*

Oscar's first bridge jump had come while using a shortcut home from school, in his coastal town in Puerto Rico. It was under the bridges where he and his friends would go to hang out as children to play music, and he'd watched all the older kids gladly make the dive into the waters so many times before.

When he was a younger that bridge seemed as if it were the only place that he and his friends could ever escape the worries of school, parents, and all the depressing newspaper articles of how the world was going further to shit.

It was a dangerous thing to jump the seventy-foot dive from the railway bridge, which had initiated Oscar as a child into more daring adrenaline rushing deeds of danger such as the one he was currently undertaking this fateful night. His father *'didn't raise no fool'* and he was a man who planned things thoroughly before he went jumping off bridges, as was taught.

This evening's job was going to be his most massive dive off the bridge of life ever, his *Magnum Opus* above all other daring accomplishments in his life. Oscar surmised that this evening was not much different from taking a risky dive off a huge bridge, and he'd found that the science of controlled freefall and daring acts of revenge, were similar to sex. If done skillfully, it could be an exhilarating experience. If done wrong, well, it could be disastrous.

But tonight he wasn't just leaping from the bridge; he was gonna blow the whole damned thing to hell and finally have his father's revenge.

Tonight was the night that the world would be set straight once more, he thought.

Oscar had been planning his scheme for almost three months now, and been fiercely yearning for this night to come for almost fifteen years. He'd begun his search for Desmond Richards's way before ever joining the Army, or even graduating high school.

Desmond became Oscar's obsession the day he'd found out that he was the man who'd killed his father, and ruined his life.

Sure, even Oscar could admit his father had been a brutal man, a gunrunner with a cruel heart of greedy ambition and a stone-cold history of dirty deeds done himself, and probably, given the opportunity, he would have done the same thing to Desmond, had he been given the chance.

That was the business of being a *Death Dealer.*

'You can trust no one,' as his father had told Oscar when he was just 18 years of age and heading out on his own into the cruel world, right before his last job with Desmond.

The job where he got 86'ed from life.

For years his desperate search to find Desmond had come up empty, but then one day, while on tour in Iraq he found himself in a fling with a very brassy female lieutenant named Lucy Turner, who had access to the new war on terror *'fuck constitutional rights'* Patriot Act databases.

Oscar had spent a few sex-hazed nights with her before one night, while spooning in bed naked together, she'd asked him, *'So what makes you a man, really?'*

Oscar joked that his manhood had already been well established with her.

Her laugh was one of the few he'd ever seen from the normally dronish and very matter of fact persona she usually portrayed to the outside world as a soldier. *'No really, what makes you tick?'* She sincerely wanted to know more about him.

So he shared himself intimately, telling the stories of his life - about his father Diego, and his obsessive lifelong search for the man responsible for taking his father from him.

Oscar remembered being floored at how easy it was for Lucy to breach protocol for him, and it had taken her literally a half-hour of the clock's time with her high security clearance to access the government's file on Desmond. Lucy had joked that 'they might not be able to find *Osama Bin Laden,* but at least the loss of *civil rights* in *America* came with a benefit for people in positions of power': *Vengeance and personal gain.*

Everything Oscar needed to pull the job was in the file: Desmond's alias, where he lived, and every job he'd ever pulled, including his entire holdings in gold, cash and diamonds. The read out sheet estimated his current value to be a very cool $20,000,000. She even included all of Desmond's cell phone calls in audio files, going back 10 years just to impress him with her access.

Then they made love in the back of a hummer.

Oscar was looking forward to looking Lucy up and partying her down when this was all over. He even fancied asking her to marry him and settle somewhere nice with kids, and to quit the war business before it killed them both.

Oscar had just been looking to get even and end the man's life, but when he realized that he could also get rich, the opportunity couldn't be passed up.

To pull off such a tediously dangerous heist he needed someone *he could trust,* and there was only one person left alive on the planet whom Oscar knew he could count on to aid him in such a risky endeavor as stealing the millions from Desmond.

Jacob Sonedo.

But everyone that knew him well just called him *Jackson,* and Oscar was glad that he was on board with him on this mission, though he was agitated and nervous about the *'wild card'* involvement of *Sheri* and had to tolerate her naively *altruistic* nature. Oscar didn't particularly care for her, never had and never would; she was too high maintenance and chatty for his tastes.

But they were a package deal; Jackson loved her and would not do the job without her. Oscar needed Jackson, and Jackson needed her, so he'd allowed her to be a part of it, reluctantly.

The Plan was unique and well thought out. Remove the cashier from the premises and go in fast and furious for the money; it wouldn't take him more than fifteen minutes to complete all that he needed to do.

Or so he'd thought.

Oscar was no stranger to the way even the best-laid plans can hurtle towards chaos at the drop of a dime, though. He had learned that life lesson way before the army, and war.

A week previous he'd snuck in during a day shift and placed a hidden camera in the office to get the safe's combination; the video footage caught Desmond's hands going through the sequence of spins and numbers, revealing the combination.

Oscar now stood in front of Desmond's huge wall safe, having picked the lock to the entrance after Rowan and the others had left the store successfully, sneaking quietly into the womb of Desmond's treasury, ready to reap the rewards of his search for personal justice. He turned his headlamp on so that he could be guided through the task of entering the combination and went through the motions; then Oscar went to pull the latch to open the door, *but it wouldn't budge.*

So he tried it again, still to find the latch wouldn't release.

On the third time of coming up empty, and discovering that there seemed to be a new combination in place, was aggravating. His hidden spy camera had been all a waste of time after all.

"It's only been a fucking week," he said to himself aloud. He was annoyed, but not enraged that Desmond had already changed the combination to the massive solid steel Diebold wall Safe that was hidden behind a swing out shelf, in the back of his office. But he knew that Desmond was a systematically cautious man by nature, and had obviously changed the combination to the safe in the past few days.

Just like his father had; *once a week, like clockwork,* probably; he should have known Desmond had the same paranoid habits as his father.

Oscar's Father, *Diego Manchez,* and *Desmond* had been partners for decades, selling illegal arms to drug dealers and tyrant dictatorships, or rebel terrorist, or whoever was buying the world over.

It didn't much matter who the buyer was to them - or what they were going to do with the weapons. Desmond and his father only cared about one thing: *they were making fortunes selling them.*

Oscar's plans of easily getting rich himself, though, had a sudden kink in it; he no longer had Desmond's combination; and there was no time left to muck around with Spyware; the game was on already. He wasn't waiting for another go at this, and he was glad that he'd come prepared. He wasn't going to let the fact that he didn't have the combo anymore stop him from attaining the wealth inside the safe; and he wasn't going to wait another hour for this to happen.

It was time to get to take drastic measures.

'Just in Case' Oscar imagined the ghost of his father whispering to him at that moment; it had been an old saying of his, when suggesting that one should bring a gun to a knife fight - and a grenade, and a bazooka... *Hell, everything and anything that would give you the advantage.*

Such were the ways of war, and the men who toil in it. *'Shut up and speak with your gunpowder,'* his father would have said if he were here now looking at the unexpected obstacle before him.

Advice that he would have gladly accepted and had come prepared to follow through on.

Oscar had been taught by his father to be prepared for as many *'Variables'* as one could think of when *'jumping off a bridge'* as this.

So, having prepared for this possibility, he reached into his black satchel latched around his shoulder, and removed a small plastic case. Kneeling down and using his headlamp to see, he opened the case to reveal several rectangular tubes of C-4 explosives and some blasting caps.

Speak? Hell, I'm ready to shout, he would tell his father if he were there now.

Oscar was a military-trained explosives expert with years of real life so called *'theater'* experience to hone his skill. So blowing this safe would be easy enough for him, he assumed, as he began estimating the amount of C-4 he would need and where it should ideally be placed for the best results.

A sudden knocking on the front door rapidly and loudly echoed through the quiet store.

It was at this very moment that *Scott Anderson*, who was known around the town of Ashton to be a very stubborn and nosey man, was hastily thumping his knuckles upon the glass, while scoping the store's dark interior for any sign of Rowan.

Oscar, startled by the arrival of such a random witness at the very moment of thinking about it, quickly turned off his headlamp and drew his Glock-9mm handgun from its holster harnessed to his right thigh. *'Just in case.'*

"*Go away now,*" Oscar whispered aloud, as he broke out in a sweat and hawkeyed the customer standing outside the door from his place in the shadows of the office's dark crevasse.

To Oscar's relief, as he watched, after a short pondering pause, that was exactly what Scott Anderson did; he went away, getting back into his car and sparking the engine, then drove away into the night.

Oscar peered at him as he left, through the window from the shadows of the dark doorway to the back office of *Conway's Quikee,* relieved that the Variable seemed small and of no further concern.

But if Oscar had known what type of person Scott Anderson was, he would have been *very concerned.* Because upon finding out that the gas station was eerily dormant, Scott did what was in his nature; he got nosey.

After coming up short knocking on the door, and leaving for another gas station 20 miles away, he immediately decided that this was as good a time as any to check in with his old buddy *Conway.* He'd heard through the grapevine that he'd had some great used hunting rifles for sale, and had been meaning to touch base with him anyways.

And so, Scott Anderson placed the fateful call to Carl Conway. The call that set Oscar's plans and his life once more adrift upon the stormy sea of entropy and poetic chaos.

Life was once again ready to remind him that the term *'nothing ever goes according to plan'* had been one carved into the minds of men for a long-long time, and for a very good reason.

It was too damn true to forget.

Oscar looked at his watch, pushing the light button on it; the time was illuminated to be to be a ghostly-neon-green *2:45 A.M.*

45 Minutes? Was Oscar's best *guesstimate.*

That's how much time he had before the local police department would be able to physically respond to any calls that would be made - *if* the explosion were to be heard or seen by any random witnesses, that is.

Oscar knew well enough from his *Special Ops* training that it's crucial to create a diversion for any local hostiles and variables that a soldier would prefer to avoid when raiding a target.

That's why just ten minutes previous he'd made a fake call about some drunken gun skirmish happening on a locally secluded beach on the fringe of the county. The location was a well-known party spot for local teens.

When the police got there, all they would find was the commotion of a bunch of drunk and horny kids, dancing to whatever music was popular. They would then spend the time rounding them up, searching for the supposed weapons and mischief-makers, and would spend the next few hours having to call their parents and filling out paperwork.

And most importantly be oblivious to the real crime. By the time they could respond to the scene, Oscar would be long gone.

After one last look over the dead and vacant parking lot for any other surprises, and finding none that he could see, Oscar rally called a passionate *"Fire in the Hole - whoo'ah,"* to the shadow of his father's ghost; the sound only fell on quietness and dark shadows.

He then swiftly got to work on fixing his slight problem, ready to punch a major hole in the silence.

2:47 A.M.

Ambulatories Spiritum Nocti

Was what was tattooed on his skin in *Latin;* it was scrawled elegantly across the back of his neck in overlapping red and black inks.

In English it roughly meant: *'GhostWalkers Of The Night'.*

'GhostWalkers' was what they'd called themselves in Iraq, during the heat of the *War on Terror.*

The Latin phrase was at the end accompanied by a round *Crest.* The symbols within the crest were made up of a key and a knife, which were crossed over a globe of the world, and it said a lot about the type of men they were.

Or at least- had once been...

Jackson and Oscar were the only ones left still walking the earth from the *GhostWalkers* Gang now.

They all hadn't been just soldiers or mercenaries – they'd fancied themselves modern Crusaders. All six of them - the Sarge, Jackson, Ron, Syd, Keith and Oscar - had bonded as blood brothers with the same tattoo after they had survived their first tour in Iraq intact.

The Sarge, Ron, Syd and Keith were all gone now, no longer here to get drunk with and watch each other's backs. Most all of them had been blown to smithereens by IED's over the last few tours - all of them except the Sarge, who took another path to the afterlife.

But Jackson and Oscar, against all odds, were still here kicking and screaming their way through life, shit poor and bitter.

Soldiers didn't return heroes anymore; Jackson wondered if they ever really did, or if it was something, they just tell us to get us to go chasing enemy shadows. Their grandfathers had fought the Nazis and returned from World War 2 flush with wealth and bravado.

Sadly, for men like him, this wasn't the case today.

What they were returning to now was a country filled with poverty and massive collective debt and stress, with no good jobs left for working men, and a populace that didn't even seem concerned - not enough anyway.

The only other person who cared about Jackson besides Oscar was Sheri, but no matter how much she loved him, it was still Oscar who was the only one who could truly understand what he'd been through, what he'd become. The only one who still had his back, protecting each other from the *'Ghost Snipers'* out there - somewhere in the war zone of life, and the only one left who didn't judge him for his sins.

Oscar and Jackson would take shifts together and would post lookouts during the war, which often meant just quietly looking at the dead lying in the streets for hours, their cold lifeless eyes staring at you, through you.

Walking with their ghosts in your mind, pacing the desert trying to understand why he was even there, having not found the promised weapons of mass destruction.

The ghouls that still haunted Jackson.

'Where was the Peace Corp now?' they had often joked about it. All they ever found was a burned out country with tired and angry people, people who needed food and not bombs, jobs and

opportunity instead of chaos and destruction.

But bullshit and bullets were his business; they were soldiers, after all.

It had become a common practice of the insurgency to use the dead as decoys, attached to *Improvised Explosive Devices,* or *IED's* as they called them, and they were everywhere, all the time - looking to *'frag us into the afterlife'.*

'Frackin' Game over...' as Sarge had put it once, using his favorite new swear variation that had recently joined pop culture dialect.

It had been war after all...

Not a Hollywood Movie with a happy ending.

Not a videogame; there were no reset buttons in real world combat...

No second chances in real life.

Jackson had learned that war was no more than one long impossibly thankless job of cleaning up the messes that out of touch power brokers had created in the first place. In the end he concluded − *'War sucks,'* as the Sarge once bluntly put it, looking for words to explain the loss of a friend and brother.

'Good things have side effects and bad things benefits,' as Oscar would always say at those moments.

Jackson often had thought it would be a good idea to have a videogame that posed the aftereffects of war, a game that worked on problem solving skills with the circumstances of refugees and starvation, instead of just warrior training, and killing. Now that game could prepare our soldiers for the modern war zones and natural disasters.

Because that's what he found real war to have been; *a thankless babysitting job with a gun.*

Except in war, the kids are shooting back at you.

How could they bring peace to the streets that were being torn apart by all the sectarian violence and fighting? The chaos and fear of uncertainty had been like a blanket over the mood of all those who lived in the war zone, suffocating them all into a droning trauma called *numbness.*

Jackson wasn't sure they had cleaned up the mess. Reading the newspapers lately made him think otherwise; in fact it seemed more like they had made a wreck instead, and it so often felt like there was no way he'd ever be able to leave the war behind; he was still living it everyday at home, still dealing with it all, as best he could.

Anyway he could.

'You call this dealing with it?!' he remembered Sheri having screamed at him one night, after he had returned from his second tour and she had seen how ugly it was getting for him to *Deal with it...*

With all the night terrors, and jittery nerves and knee jerk reactions to the smallest things, and the panic-

The *Sarge* would only tell them, all of them, to just *'suck it up'* and they only had a little longer before they would be home and safe with their loved ones, and *all would be okay.*

But Jackson knew that *it was not all-okay...*

But the Sarge knew nothing he could say to them would make any of the horror disappear. He knew there really were no glorious pep talks that could make the insanity of war cease to haunt them all.

It bothered everyone; *that's why no one ever talked about it.*

That's why the Sarge would just do the clichéd *'whoo'ah'* rally cry and add the regular pre-rehearsed *'Suck it up speech.'*

That is, before the Sarge blew his brains out one day, deciding to suck up a bullet instead; he was tired of telling them all to just *'suck it up'* Jackson guessed.

He remembered thinking, after seeing the Sarge's dead body lying in the sand, his life taken by his own hand and will, that he couldn't call him a coward.

Jackson couldn't blame the Sarge for not having anything better to tell them all about dealing with Post Traumatic Stress Disorder. Guilt tinged him; he regretted that he didn't see the Sarge was just as bad off as he was - worse it turns out, actually.

He often wondered if there had been something – anything - that he could have done or said to help the Sarge.

Hell, Jackson didn't know what to say to anybody, *not even himself...*

Whoever did about such deep tragedy?

When he'd been trying to figure out how he could help Sherri deal with his P.T.S.D., he'd found it was often just easier for everyone else not to talk about it, as if not speaking of it would make it go away.

But the *'Ghost Light'* was always there for him.

Like it was now, glowing from the park lamp that was perched upon a pole thirty yards away. It was the kind of light-glow that haunted him madly; the kind that sent *panic attacks raging into his soul.*

The crick in his back was the first sign that one was creeping in slowly; he could feel it tightening on him, closing in, like *'a sledgehammer to the chest,'* as his sergeant would often call it in Afghanistan on his third tour when the fits had gotten really bad.

The thunder and lightning continued to infuse the clouds with fury over the ocean, as Jackson's beer induced urge to urinate had led him to wander towards the tree line with his brooding mind running rampant.

Right near where Vang was hidden, having followed Rowan and the two strangers to the park, and having managed to park his car at the entranceway to the cliffs without having been noticed by them.

Jackson unzipped his pants and pulled out his little soldier and began shooting the grass with it's fizzling stream of warm piss.

As Vang quietly watched, nervous about how close the stranger had wandered towards his hiding place in the bushes. His father and grandfather had always talked about the way of the hunt, as they had often reminisced about jungle living; they would always remind him as a boy that one must be silent, and go unnoticed, to be most effective.

This is what Vang was trying to do - go unnoticed, and be silent - and he was doing it well enough.

That is until the flash of lightning lit up the sky and penetrated the brush, causing a sparkle off the metal zipper on Vang's sweatshirt. *This is what caught Jackson's eye;* sending his warrior instincts on end. When Jackson saw the twinkle from the brush, he'd been half done with relieving his bladder. His urine sprayed to mist in the rowdy winds, wetting the swaying hay that was hissing at his feet.

Jackson's attention honed in on the position of interest; his senses began to tingle fiercely. Then, gazing around the park and noticing that a car was parked near the entrance, he began to fear that he had something new to worry about. The vehicle was coyly placed on the side of the road near a small gathering of trees on the cliffs, about one hundred yards away, and had not been there when they entered, he was sure of that.

They no longer appeared to be alone.

Jackson's nerves jolted, as he put all of his attention on the area the glisten had come from. Trees and shrubs didn't sparkle.

Sure, it could just be a piece of trash, an old beer can or some plastic bag. *But it could also be 'a whoop ass surprise'* as the *Sarge* would call the moment of being ambushed by enemy fighters.

His P.T.S.D triggered.

That bomb-blast-ear-shock sound took hold of Jackson like a humming thunder; it was a pinging ring in his inner ear, or his head, or his imagination as some clueless army shrinks often suggested- it didn't matter where it came from; it would just come - and when it did come over him, he got sick quick.

It was like the world was closing in on him; he would get claustrophobic even when standing in wide-open spaces, like now.

It was like being possessed by a demon.

Jackson began to feel dizzy and reckless as the *'Ringing sound of the howling dead'* sang like sirens in his cranium, driving him into madness.

Perhaps that's the last thing the Sarge heard before he went to the afterlife? Jackson had wondered often when the attacks came over him.

But that was not his concern right now, as his focus targeted in on the tree line, his ears ringing bomb-shock in the background of his skull getting ever louder by the moment.

The trees, with their rattling leaves in the swaying branches, rampaging in the rush of the storm, made a swishing orchestra of sound as they were whistled in the wind. The way the trees were *'ghost lit'* by the one street lamp from the parking lot gave Jackson a very edgy feel, and a cold shiver trembled through his body and mind.

It was the kind of *'Ghost Light'* that Jackson had spent a lot of time under when patrolling the streets of Baghdad.

They called it the *'Ghost Light'* because that was the way that Baghdad had been lit during the long night-shifts they'd pulled for years. Those nights had been dubbed the *'killing hours'* while they were on tour through Iraq's shattered streets, where he'd been, with Oscar, an I.E.D first responder.

Jackson and Oscar had both been members of an elite team of bomb specialists whose job was to find and disable all land mines and *Improvised Explosive Devices* the enemy had littered around Iraq.

And these had been anywhere and everywhere, and when not discovered – brutally fatal and tragic.

Their patrols over those years had been relentless, and at times, it seemed never ending - Responding to call after grizzly call of insanity of the first degree would eventually break even the hardest shell of any person. His unit had been tight; they all had each other's back, and had tried to stay focused to the missions at hand. But one by one, they all began to fracture under the pressure through the years, including Jackson.

"I'm like fucking Humpty-Dumpty...' He would try to explain to Sheri. Jackson's shell was cracked, he knew it, perhaps even shattered, and she was desperately trying to glue him back together. Buildings could be renovated and rebuilt after war; but people's hearts and minds - and the societies they lived in - were much harder to fix once they'd been shattered and broken down.

They truly loved each other, Sheri and Jackson, and it was their mutual concern that was the only thing that got him out of bed anymore.

It certainly wasn't a job, something he was currently lacking.

He'd found several times over since returning from his tours that employers just didn't care much to have a man on the payroll that was viewed as *'Damaged Goods,'* as he'd often been called. Usually by the same pencil pushers who so fervently applauded his march off to war in the *'fight for freedom'* ironically enough.

The same people were now calling men like him *'Liabilities'* and always looking to sweep them under the rug - to *'free'* them from employment - not wanting to be bothered with the social ramifications and costs of war.

'Out of sight is out of mind' was the way of business and politics, his father had often remarked of such things.

But right now Jackson's senses were screaming to him to be mindful of what was out of sight, as the conversation between Cindy/Sheri and Rowan continued.

"Did you know that most of the stars out there in the sky are binary sun systems?"

"What's bi-*anally*?" Cindy asked, being, well, a *wise-ass*.

Rowan laughed at Cindy's intended mispronunciation, easing into the conversational distraction. "It means they have two suns. Our solar system is actually a peculiarity in the universe with only one sun."

"Really? Jackson, did you hear that? We're all *peculiarities*." She laughed, looking over to him peeing, then noticed that he was preoccupied with looking into the shadows of the trees on the edge of the field and was not at all paying attention to them.

"See how smart she is?" she said to him trying to get his attention.

Jackson was still ignoring her.

So Cindy, taking a drag from her smoke, turned back to Rowan and declared to her, "I bet you're going to love college."

"I did love it... Too bad I'm not ever going back."

"Really? Why not?"

"I can't afford it..." said Rowan; tired of telling people the reason.

"That's just not right. What about scholarships, and college loans and stuff?"

"I've been trying. But so far what little I could get still wasn't enough to keep me there."

"Now that's not right. With all the money our government spends bailing out rich people, and the wars, you'd think they'd have enough left over to send a smart pretty thing like you to college?"

"You'd think..." She agreed wholeheartedly.

Cindy turned to see that Jackson was still

looking toward the trees. "What are you doing?"

Jackson still didn't pay her any attention; it was all focused on the field's edge.

"Oh shit; I know that look." Cindy got up, concerned, and joined Jackson as he scoped the shadowy edge of the tree line. She was clearly worried as she approached him, then grabbing his arm to rip his attention back to her, she gently asked him "What is it this time?"

"I don't know, I thought I saw something." Usually it was nothing, at least since he had been home in America, that is.

But he couldn't resist the tingles of danger and fear, they were why he was still kicking and breathing, he believed. He had learned long ago ignoring these intuitions was a bad idea.

"You're just a little jumpy is all? I'm sure it's nothing, like usual..." As she said this, a fallen tree branch could be heard crackling under Vang's shifting footsteps in the brush.

Jackson's was on, and he sprang forth like a viper into action, pulling a pistol from his pants.

Rowan and Cindy were both thrown into excitement and fear as they watched Jackson charge the edge of the *'Ghost-Lit'* tree line relentlessly, as he had been trained and conditioned to do.

As was his beastly nature now.

Jackson pointed the gun into the contours of the trees on the edge of the field and yelled out to the person that he knew was hiding there: "*Very slowly*, I want you to remove yourself from the shadows, with your hands reaching for the sky; *like a lightning rod* I want you to reach up as you come out; you hear me?!"

He spoke this with an ice-cold hiss that sent shivers through Cindy and Rowan.

The shadows were quiet; except for the rumbling thunder and the wind rustling the trees, but still no signal that anyone was there.

This time he spoke with even more hostility than before. "I want to hear from you! *Otherwise* I'm gonna strike you with *my* lightning..." He motioned his gun in a quick wave toward the shadows to make his point clear enough, "*Do you got it?!..*"

Suddenly Vang's voice could be heard calling out from the shadows of the trees. "Don't shoot! I'm coming out, alright..."

"Get your ass out here now!"

"Just relax, Okay? I'm coming!"

"You're the one who needs to get your ass out of them trees *so I can relax*!" Jackson coldly stated, trying to keep his finger from twitching and adding more tragedy to the world.

Vang, with his hands held high as commanded, exited from his hiding spot in the trees cautiously.

Jackson saw he had no gun, and did not look like a cop or the thug type, so he began to ease up a little on his fury. "*Who are you?!*" He demanded.

Vang is a little taken back by the sudden interrogation and mortal danger of the situation. "My name's Vang Cha."

Rowan instantly recognized him. "Vang? Thank god you're here."

"You know him?" Jackson asked, not at all turning his gaze away from the sudden intruder, his gun steadily pointed, ready to shoot at any provocation. "Well, Mister Cha, *what the hell you doing sneaking up on us like that for?!"*

"I didn't think I was sneaking up on you; this is a public park you know..." Vang hoped his bluff was good enough, but just in case, added, "I was just out visiting this place to watch the lightning is all."

"He's just a freaking kid; look at him... So, just chill the fuck out. Okay?" Cindy pleaded to her man in a calm voice; she'd found out yelling at him only made things worse...

"Yeah, hey Rowan, how strange seeing you here; I thought you were working..."

He laughed nervously, realizing that last tidbit might have tipped his hand that he knew something sketchy seemed to be going on.

"Hi..." Cindy wanted to try and break the arctic frigidness in the air, and went to shake Vang's hand.

Vang looked over toward the man holding a gun at him to see if it was okay for him to move.

Jackson looked over at Rowan, then back to Vang, and then said, "Well, go on now, and don't be rude. Shake the woman's hand..."

Vang did as requested and reached his arms down, greeting her friendship happily with his right hand, hoping that there would be more good will to follow.

Jackson, still holding the gun firmly in his hand, though not directly at the shaken young man standing before him, looked over at Rowan, who was standing, very stunned, a few feet away, and asked her, "So we're cool, right?"

"What's wrong with you? Yeah of course, we're cool. He's my friend. Why wouldn't we be cool?"

Cindy, knowing that Rowan's angst filled tone of voice only seemed to unhinge him further; saw the situation was stressing him into *'The Panic Zone'* and that he was on the verge of another nervous breakdown, or flashback, or whatever it was that struck Jackson at times like these.

'P.T.S.D's a bitch to deal with' she remembered the army psychologist telling her in a family counseling session once, right after listing off a bunch of therapies that could help him, the only catch being that the army didn't cover such expensive procedures, that is, if you could even *prove* that he was sick in the first place. The Government's official standing towards vets filing for ailments, they'd discovered to their astonishment, was that they must be lying, making it up, and the amount of agency runaround for filing was infuriatingly complex.

In the end, they were on their own, they'd heartbreakingly found.

They had taken her lover off to war and broke him, and now that he'd returned, they couldn't even bother to help glue him back together. *'Life's a bitch'* was all the therapist could say to her about the wrangling ordeal of trying to get aid from the Government to pay for his medical needs.

Her mind quickly ran through the list of methods she'd tried to console him when he got like this, and there had been only one surefire ploy that worked. Only one thing that she'd discovered tamed his beast, one action she could do to take command of this ship and sail his mood away from jagged rocks, away from the sirens in his head. She could see the panic swelling within him, and knew there was only one thing that could be done about it. All she could do to help him vent off his steam, before it blew up in a violent way; *was to give him a blowjob.*

It always did the trick; of all the things she'd tried, it could best rein Jackson's mood away from the volcanic temper that would erupt.

"Put the fucking gun away, and come with me right now." She said sternly, and then got tender, as she pleaded with him in her loving voice, with her best sexy eyes. "You need to rein it in, soldier; you need to come back to me, okay. Look at me..."

He looked into her eyes, "I'm looking..."

"Good... Everything is gonna be okay," she told him, and then kissed his cheek lovingly. This got him to finally put the gun away, having been soothed by her.

Cindy then turned toward Rowan and Vang apologetically, saying, "I'm sorry, guys. He has this condition that makes him ah'little jumpy. Excuse us for a moment; and I'll put him straight again."

Taking Jackson's hand, she led him toward the trees just a few yards away. "Let's tame this dragon right now."

Rowan and Vang watched as they went off together, wondering what would happen next.

Cindy and Jackson disappeared into the shadows, and immediately went at it.

Rowan and Vang both listened as Cindy gave a moaning Jackson instant relief.

She turned to Vang, who had a perplexed and eerie look on his face, as they shared an uncontrollable giggle at the mutual realization that what they were hearing was exactly what they thought it was.

Wow, that's a girl who knows how to take action. Rowan admired that about Cindy in the moment, grateful she had defused Jackson's frightening angst.

Vang's hilarious smile suddenly turned gray when he remembered the seriousness of the moment. *"What is going on here?* Rowan, I thought you were working?"

"Have you heard about the tsunami?" Glad that he was now safe with her, or at least he thought. Suddenly she got a flashing thought - what the world might look like after the wave had struck. *'Hurricane Katrina'...* Or worse, *'Fukishima',* is what the world would look like afterwards, she guessed fearfully.

"What?!" Vang replied, taken aback, this being the first he'd heard of such a thing.

Rowan was snapped herself once again into the moment's pertinent danger, the *Tsunami.* She informed him of what she knew so far. "There was an earthquake, and there is a Tsunami warning in effect; that's why we're here, to escape the wave..."

Vang was shocked by the revelation. "I didn't hear anything about it on the radio on the way over here. When did this happen?"

"Uh, I guess about ah'half hour ago? Maybe." Suddenly a spark of hope struck her morose pose. "Vang; Do you have a cell phone? I lost mine on the way here, and everyone is sleeping. I need to warn people."

"Yeah, it's right here," he told her, happy to help. Astounded at the gravity of the news of an impending natural disaster headed towards them at the very moment, he retrieved the phone from his jeans and handed it to her.

Rowan was excited to get to the phone. "Oh! You are my hero." Immediately dialing her parents number, she hears it begin ringing.

"Do you have any loved ones around the eastern coastlines?" Rowan asked Vang, as the phone continued to ring at her parents' house.

"Not family, though I have plenty of friends; I go to school in Boston-"

"Mom, Dad, you have to wake up right now!" was the message she left them when it went to the answering machine.

At this very moment, Jackson's *tension massage* that he had been receiving from Cindy came to its tremendous climax, as he bellowed a gasping, "*Uuhhhhhh!*"

'*My therapy prescription*' for soldiers encountering P.T.S.D. could revolutionize counseling, she smirked to herself. Cindy wondered what the army would think if she proposed that as an official vet insured and covered treatment.

She had the far-fetched idea of being awarded a Nobel peace prize for finally having discovered the cure to Post Traumatic Stress Disorder.

Blowjobs not Bombs!

Would be the cute motto for her Not-For-Profit Foundation, which could service the world, she mockingly imagined.

Jackson's relief was momentary. The rush subsiding now, he looked out to notice that Rowan had a phone in her hand, *and worse yet,* he screamed in his thoughts, *she's just made a phone call to someone!*

Cindy was still dreaming about how she was finally learning how to calm *his demons wa-*

"Frack! The *kid* had a phone, Sherri!" He panicked immediately.

Shit, the Demons are back, Cindy thought to herself, watching as he began to whip his mood into irritability again, like lightning storming back. *Goodbye Nobel Peace-*

Jackson didn't wait around to hear her response, pulling his gun once more he sprang his thunder through the tree brush and out onto the field, his feet *swishing* through the tall-uncut hay grass, which was thigh-high on his charging stampede.

"Sweetie! Stop! Calm Down, please! Jacob!" Cindy's pleas were not even heard; *Jackson was on a mission.*

As the wind began to kick up a fury as rain drops sprayed from the convoluting clouds overhead, the storm announced its arrival with a bright flashing bolt of lightning, which struck a tree with a crashing boom just 150 yards from them.

Jackson's nerves were lit on fire, as he instinctively dove towards the ground, to safety, as his flashback mentality triggered his reaction to duck for cover from such a loud and sudden sound. The bomb flash effect of the lightning didn't help either.

Jackson's fingers went primal, and a few rounds were fired compulsively from his gun in response to the sudden intrusion of the storm's chaos.

No bullets struck anyone.

"I'm so sorry. Sometimes he gets a little kooky is all," Cindy called out to Rowan and Vang as she chased after Jackson to try to stop him from doing something stupid.

Jackson, realizing it was just a tree that was struck by lightning, and was not a bomb, jumped back to his feet quickly, and towards Vang and Rowan he went, his gun sprung with his right hand, his face a manic filled canvas of confusion and mayhem. Threatened by the young adults; somehow, for some reason, yet again.

Rowan and Vang, upon seeing Jackson once more carrying danger their way, with his pistol taking charge, both instinctively began to back away.

Rowan's foot was snagged on a rock; she tumbled to the ground backwards, and Vang nobly tried to help her back onto her feet, but it was too late.

Jackson was already towering aggressively over them, with his *Glock-9mm pistol* held firmly in his nervous palm.

Right on his tail is Cindy, who approached with the cunning of a person cautiously stepping around a wild and dangerous beast.

Rowan admired the Lion Tamer in her, as Cindy made her way apprehensively to stand in between Jackson and them.

"We agreed we were not going to be like this anymore... No more collateral damage, right?"

Jackson looked into the calming eyes of her caring gaze. "I'm trying love... But damn'it what do you expect me to do?" He loosened his trepidation for the moment, pointing his gun towards the ground instead.

"Not this..." she said, her words twinged with despondency. "So just cool your jets babe, please..."

Cindy then shifted her hips to face towards Rowan and Vang. "The war... You know... Post

106

Traumatic Stress Disorder and all, makes him a little edgy in this kind of light is all," she tried to explain to them apologetically. "He's getting *better, though*. And everything's going to be okay..." Cindy hoped; but was beginning to wonder.

"*This* is getting better?" Rowan asked her, thunderstruck. Terrified that she was amongst such wildly hell-bent company.

"Things are getting better... They really *are...*" she half-heartedly reassured them. *"They* are..."

Then, switching gears, Cindy said to them, "*Hey,* you should both have a beer with us and relax. Don't worry about the phone right now; everything will be alright, just trust me..." as if nothing had happened at all.

Rowan is caught off guard by the sudden shifting of the situation's threatening nature. "What's going on here?" she demanded from them.

"Forget about making any more phone calls right now. Okay?" Jackson said flatly, as he forcefully searched Vang's pockets, and finding only his car keys, took them from him as well. Vang wasn't in a position to argue about it, so he said nothing.

"Why?" Rowan dared to question.

Jackson looked at both of them, his gun still held ready to be used.

"Just have a beer with us..." it being more of a demand than a suggestion., as he stepped forward and coldly leered towards Vang and Rowan in a beastly way.

Suddenly *Rowan's* phone began to ring from inside Cindy's purse.

Rowan immediately recognized the ring-tone as hers. "You've had my phone this whole time?"

Her phone continued to sing its ring-tone cyclically as they all stood quietly, collectively feeling the tension of the shifting situation.

Rowan audaciously demanded answers, *"What is going on?!"*

Cindy and Jackson gave each other a shared look of disappointment that everything was unraveling rapidly, as Rowan's phone went to voicemail.

Jackson walked up to Vang and looked him in the eye; a silent danger could be seen, shouting loudly in his mean glare, as the winds pushed upon them all a hard gush.

"*Now,* give me the phone."

Vang relinquished his phone to Jackson without further discussion.

"Now; you can tell us *who* you just called?"

Rowan, realizing that she was too young to die, oddly heard just one thing, though, *the radio*: with its mellow Jazz music that was wafting from Jackson's car -completely contradictory to the moment's perilous complexity - as a deep soulful woman's voice gently bellowed a sassy melody, singing about how *love broke her heart.*

Rowan feared that her heart would die - before ever truly knowing love...

2:59 A.M.

Carl Conway, having just gotten off the phone with his old friend Scott, and wondering why the store was currently dormant, was trying to get in touch with Rowan. After having failed to get her on the store's landline, he was now attempting to reach her on her cell.

But again, she did not respond, and he only got her voice mail.

"You've reached the automated message depot for Rowan Ellian, so speak to the machine, and the real me will get back to you when I can." Carl was perplexed, finding it strange that she didn't answer her phone.

She was a young American girl, after all.

'*She must sleep with the damned thing,*' he often joked to his buddies.

Conway had the twirling idea for a while now that Rowan's phone probably got more action than he'd had from his wife in a long time.

Beep went the recorder on Rowan's Voicemail.

"Rowan, yeah I just got a call from Simon. He said he drove by the store and the place was dark and closed up? What's going on? Give me a call damn'it..." Conway did not like it one bit that she did not answer her phone. He knew she was young and restless, but one thing she wasn't - was irresponsible.

The sense that something was wrong began to tug at his mind. *I should have taught her how to shoot a gun* is a thought that came to him, as he hoped his money was okay...

He muddled in his mind all the possible things that could be responsible for Rowan's sudden roguery.

Conway made swift his mission to get to the bottom of it all.

He put his coat on and headed for the door in a hurry; he stopped as he was halfway out, and turned to the cabinet by the door on his left.

Quickly he swung open the wooden hatch and pulled from its interior a *Magnum-44,* which was already loaded; Carl always had his guns ready to go, always...

'*Just in case,*' he thought.

It was *Carl Conway's* black-market slogan, after all. That was the line that his goon-customers ate up like hotcakes. The saying had made him a filthy rich man. Back when his name had been *Desmond Richards.*

3:00 A.M.

"Right now - There is a wave of tribulation on its way towards us." Jackson said this with the conviction of a man who has seen hell. "As we speak, a destructive force greater than you and I is at work – now, you can call it the hand of god, or an act of nature, whatever flushes your crap - but, trust me, it's coming, and you don't want to be in its way when it gets here... And if *you're lying* to me, and *trouble* comes of it? Then when that apocalypse arrives and you need my help – and you will - it won't be there. So, know that you were warned, and don't come begging to me for *mercy*, 'cause I will be fresh out'ah it... Trust me; you don't want to see how powerful my Armageddon can be. We clear?"

The lightning and thunder highlighted the turbulence of his words; Jackson couldn't have waited for a better moment to deliver that oration of fear into their hearts.

Vang and Rowan realized the reservoir of creepy went very deep with Jackson. They both wanted out *now* and *bad*, but unfortunately, this carnival ride wasn't stopping any time soon.

"Are you sure that you didn't call *anyone* else?!" He wanted, *needed* every ounce of information about the new variable of the call made from Vang's phone while – *they had been busy.*

Rowan, shivering in the pouring rain, screamed at him, "Yes!"

Jackson, unsure of what type of yes it was, asked, "Yes - *you did?*"

"No- Yes, *I did not* call anyone else - they're sleeping still; I didn't   even talk to them.   I swear..." Rowan hoped the interrogation was over, but the look on Jackson's face told her otherwise.

Vang and Rowan found themselves gasping for each other's comfort, as they leaned against each other, as if to get each other's back.

Cindy stepped in and pushed him aside, unafraid of the barbarian. "Jackson, you're being an ass!" She then attempted to break the tension and smiled at the two asphyxiated from the shock of Jackson's rage, and she asked them jovially, "Want a beer?"

Rowan and Vang didn't know what to say.

Jackson turns to Cindy, annoyed for butting in; she just looked at him with arms akimbo and then waved her hand dismissively at him. "Well, what do you want me to do? What?! I'm trying to save them from doing something stupid, Jackson, and without terrifying them any more than's needed. So just step the fuck back! Okay!?"

"Well what do you want me to do? Huh?!" Jackson paced like a stallion fenced in.

"I don't know, Do something besides being a giant ass. How about that?" She almost cried to him, wanting to forgive, but needing him to calm down.

Jackson looked up at the sky and matched its fury with a low, bellowous, "Great, all this for nothing... *He's* not gonna like this one bit **Sheri!**"

Vang and Rowan both simultaneously caught that Jackson actually slipped '*Cindy's*' real name in their conversation, and now both begin to wonder who **he** - is?

Cindy, without much concern about what *he* would think about anything, said, "Fuck him - *He* won't ever have to know..."

Jackson didn't like how casual she was about it; he realized that she had no clue the monster Oscar could be. Jackson himself sometimes wondered, *especially these days,* if *he* even knew *Oscar* all that well.

Hell, Jackson wondered if he even recognized *himself* anymore either, for that matter.

But Jackson knew one thing for sure; Oscar was on a warpath - and collateral damage had never been much of a concern of his - ever.

Oscar's callous indifference to people getting caught in the crossfires of a mission, *even if innocent and unprovoked,* was the kind of attention most soldiers would give to a *Moth* being burnt in the trap of an electronic bug-catcher.

Oblivious.

It had been a way of thinking that he'd witnessed at its most horrifying extremes - on many occasions.

Way too many occasions – way, way too many, Jackson thought to himself.

He believed it to be a trait that Oscar had gotten from his father, *Diego,* but also a mindset that he'd meditated on like a *Dark Monk* - or a *Sith-Lord* - since he went to war.

It was the kind of thinking that Jackson was trying to escape before it killed him, or, he even feared, Sheri too.

"You don't know him..." he said anxiously, trying to find the right way to express what Oscar could be like – at times like these anyways. "He's good at sniffing all this kind of stuff out on his own - *like* he's psychic or what not... He's *like? –* Uh fucking Sherlock Holmes hound-dog that breeded with a werewolf - kind of shit. Do you *get* me?!"

Rowan asked Cindy, or Sheri - or whoever she was, "Excuse me... **Who's** not gonna like *what?* What's happening here? There's no *Tsunami* is there - **Sheri?**" daring to say her slipped first name, and not realizing how dumb it might have actually have been to acknowledge she heard it.

That is, until she saw Jackson's *reaction* tell her how stupid it was, as he immediately began pacing again. His inner stallion was ready to jump the fence and go *off the reservation* when he realized that *he'd been the one* to divulge Sheri's name accidentally to them just a moment before.

It was *not good* that they now knew Sheri's *real* name. Only five or six people on the planet knew him as *'Jackson,'* and none of them would tell that to anyone in law enforcement.

But now that they knew that Sheri's name wasn't Cindy? Well, it wasn't good. It complicated things, a lot. *"Awe fuck!"*

"It's not *my f*ault." **Cindy / Sheri** defended herself before Jackson could blame her for it.

"I know it's my own damned fault!" Jackson growled with another round of pacing, his ears beginning to ring the sound of black-hole stress again.

Sheri turned toward Rowan to address her *very untimely* question. "No – there's no Tsunami. Your family will be fine. So you can stop worrying about that."

Vang, without skipping a beat, blurted out, *"Yeah,* right now; I think we're more worried about ourselves..."

Rowan couldn't have expressed how she was feeling any better, so she didn't even try.

Sheri reached down towards Jackson's twelve-Pack of *Magic Hat* beer lying in a muddy puddle near the rock at her feet, taking two bottles from the soaking wet card board box. She then gestured for them to each take one. "Sit with us and drink some beer – and don't worry; everything will be okay. You'll see..."

Rowan stepped pleadingly toward Sheri, not at all interested in a beer. "So Cindy – or Sheri – or whatever you want to be called - tell me why the mood really adjusted here, and I mean the super-scary kind of skew – and I'm more interested in the Truth right now; and not a beer. *Okay? So, can you just tell us what is going on here? Please?!*"

"I'm sorry I just can't do that..." Sheri was matter of fact about that, but trying to find a balance to her *personal pledge* to be *Altruistic*, she tried to soften the scary uncertainty and stress of the situation as best she could by adding, "Soon enough though – you'll have your phone back, and be free to go."

Seeing by their faces that she had not convinced Vang and Rowan that everything was okay, Sheri very sternly stomped her foot in a puddle; it splashed up upon the case of beer at her feet.

Rowan goes to say something-

Sheri's patience was wearing thin with their questions. "Look - everything will be okay – you'll just have to trust me... *Can you do that for me?* Huh guys? *Just – Trust* me?..."

Rowan and Vang cannot.

Rowan, trying to be like a *Lion Tamer*, lashed the whip of her tongue once more. "Why are we your hostages all of a sudden?"

"You're not hostages- you're gonna have to just trust me - you're being cared for, really you are..."

Almost as fast as she had asked the question, the answer hit her brain like the lightning in the sky, "Oh my god. You're robbing the store; *aren't you?*"

Sheri was impressed at how quick-minded Rowan was, and right now very annoyed by it. Sheri never had envisioned hostages being so - *mouthy, and smart.*

So, Sheri did at this moment the best thing she could think of; she tried to distract them by attempting to change the conversation once more. "*You're not hostages;* just fucking trust me and stop asking all these damned questions. Now, drink a fucking beer with us...

Jackson was not impressed that their cover was so quickly crumbling; he was beginning to feel dread burn his thoughts again. His wet clothes were beginning to give him jungle fever, *itching him bad.* Jackson's instinctive alarm set in again; when he saw Sheri's panicked reaction to the way the plan was not going as hoped. The poor kids still had *no idea* how dangerous things just got for them, so he felt he needed to make it *very clear* to them *once more - who was really in charge*, and swiftly had his gun drawn as a tool of intimidation to shut them up. "*This* is exactly what's happening right now. *Do you get it?*"

"There you go again with the threats." Sheri had her hands tossed to the thunderous sky - at wits' end with his need to use the gun. "*Jesus Christ,* can you stop with the whole *Scarface* act already?! *It's kind'ah wearing very thin with me right now Jackson...* We agreed not to play it like this."

Jackson was never a good actor anyways; it was always just too much – pressure for him. He was glad to be done with the charade part of the night. But he was now fearfully pondering the *ramifications* of the sudden, and numerous - *complications*. "Sweetie, the show's over. They can't leave. So, I guess that *is* exactly what they are; *hostages*. So, yeah, If it quacks like a duck? Well then it's a frackin' duck..."

Cindy did not like Jackson upending her attempt to calm the situation, "Jackson! Why do you always have to go jumping on the gun with everything?"

"Because it's the easiest way to get results, *that's why!*"

"But it ain't necessarily always the *right way*... We need to be *Altruistic* honey." Cindy put her hand lovingly on his shoulder, once again trying to soothe the beast with some kind of music.

Jackson had *had it* with Sheri's *Altruism* kick, and finally expressed what he had not had the balls to say - until now, about the book she read about some mathematician's quest to prove that *Altruism exists,* "Remember, the mother-fucking-dude killed himself? *He fucking killed himself* with all that *Altruism shit*. So, I don't want to hear any more about it. Alright?"

Sheri tried to remind him of their promise to each other, that no one would get hurt. "We are here because we *were* trying to do this the *right way*."

Jackson only knew the way of the gun; Sheri knew it, too. "What do you want from me? I'm giving you *all I got* baby, and it's just never good enough for you..."

Cindy felt his pain and realized that their

bickering was distracting them both from the mission at hand. "I'm sorry, you're right... Let's not fight right now."

Jackson, relieved a bit to hear her say that, gleefully huffed, *"Damned straight let's not..."*

Then the two of them, having agreed, turned their combined focus back towards Rowan and Vang.

Jackson was the first to speak. "Now - look. If you do *anything* at all to make me twitch unkindly, well, that would be your fault, which is how I'd look at it... So just cooperate with us from here on out without anymore questions and wiseass remarks or statements..."

Sheri: "I can't say much. But I will say this; you're way better off here, with us right now, than you would be back at that gas station."

Rowan: "What the hell does that mean? You people are nuts, *aren't you?"*

Sheri didn't like being called *nuts;* she never did, so she snapped back at Rowan, impatient with her need to speak her mind so freely. "No we're not! *We're your mother-fucking guardian angels! And* we're sticking *our asses* out for *you* right now, so you best be grateful."

Vang found this statement absurd. "How is that possible?"

"Even though it doesn't feel like it right now, *you have to understand;* I'm the only thing standing between you going home safely tonight, or just ending up another tragic newspaper clipping in tomorrow's press..." Sheri offered them both the beers once more, and sternly suggested. "Now drink this, don't worry - and all will be golden..."

Rowan and Vang were both in a mental state of *shock and awe* at how the night was unfolding, *to say the least.* And *to say the most* would fill a book as large as the entire unabridged version of the bible, but *one word* summed it up best.

Speechless.

3:03 A.M.

The gas station was dark, the closed sign was on the entrance, hanging tilted in the metal-framed glass door, and the mood was eerily quiet.

Until headlights beamed on the road leading toward the store, as Carl Conway made his way to his business establishment, on a mission to find the underlying cause of the night's mischief.

As his Truck approached the front of the gas station, a large explosion went off in the shop's back office, sending all sorts of debris shooting through the store.

The explosion was so fierce that it blew the office door clean from its hinges, flinging it out through the front window of the gas station in one huge crash, and out onto the hood of Carl Conway's Truck in the parking lot.

Carl's windshield shattered, as he was horrified by the sudden fury of his store blowing up, and the door landing on his truck.

"What the fuuuck!" He growled back at the sudden scare. Carl's first thoughts were that the dynamite he had stored in his office had gone sour and somehow had been setoff.

This was not good.

Conway needed help with this situation; lucky for him he had the local Police in his pocket, and he was immediately on his cell phone; he got the local county Police dispatcher.

"Kim, yeah hi, it's Carl Conway. Tell Carlson to send the boys down here immediately, my god damned store just got blown to hell."

He then hung up the phone, quickly got out of the truck, and ran to the store's entrance. He looked at the damage to the storefront, with smoke billowing from its shattered window.

Conway stood overwhelmed, as smoke billowed out the broken window; he pulled on the door, and it was locked. He reached quickly for his keys but found they were not in his pockets, as he had forgotten them at home in his rush out the door.

Without a moment's hesitation, though, he jumped through the bomb-shattered window and into the Smokey and blown out store, where he stumbled and ended up falling onto the floor with a thump, not being the fit marauder of his younger days any more.

"Hello! Is anybody in here? Rowan!?" Carl called out to the bone chillingly quiet darkness.

Silence was the only response, besides some crackling fire that was burning off the mangled hard maple door that had been torn to kindling by the blast. At this moment, some potato chip bags shuffled to the floor in one massive wave of crinkling foil.

Slightly spooked by this scene, Conway began to move toward the office. Grabbing a Fire extinguisher on his way, he used it on the light remnants of flames scattered around the store's interior and on the door leading his way to the Smokey office.

"Rowan?! What the hell have ya' done to my store?!" Carl growled out to her as he approached the back office.

Carl's warrior senses began to tingle, and he slowly pulled out his Magnum-44 and turned on the nightlight scope attached to it for light.

Carl scoped his gun around the room with his light, his grip steady on the handle of the gun, his fingers well flexed and ready. His search of the room brought him upon the sight of his *Diebold* wall safe with its door blown off and lying on the floor at his feet, and a huge pile of *money* and *gold bars* spilling from it and onto the floor. The wealth of the safe was immense; between the gold and the money, there was a few million dollars worth of loot.

$7,893,543.00, to be exact, at Carl's last count.

Carl stood in front of the money and Gold Bars heaped on the ground from the busted safe, and began to understand what was happening.

But it was too late.

From the shadows beside him sneaked-up Oscar, who floated from the Smokey murkiness, holding his gun to Conway's head like a ninja, quiet and unseen.

In his peripheral vision, Carl suddenly saw the ghostly figure holding a gun to his head. "What the-"

"Pretty cool, huh?" Oscar said to him, dressed in black and with gloves on his hands, his face slightly smudged from ash.

Carl was startled by the voice so close to him. He turned to see the gun pointed towards his head. "Uh, Not really..."

"Oh that's right... Because I got my gun to 'yer fat fucking head."

Oscar, as usual, was tripped up on what to say at this moment; he pondered saying something similar to that character in *Princess Bride* who had chased the man with six fingers: *"You killed my father blah-blah-blah."*

But it was too cliché.

Oscar, though, now found that he really was at a loss as to what he would say, now that it was upon him. He was a soldier and not a poet after all, and words were a secondary concern to a man like Oscar; the thing that spoke loudest for men like him was guns and fists.

"So, where do we go from here?" Conway asked nervously, as he turned his head to finally see who has a gun to his head.

"Do you recognize me, huh *um'bray?*" Oscar chided him with the smile of a *Walking Ghost.*

Instantly he saw the younger apparition of a long dead person, almost the spitting image of a man whose life he helped end - *Diego Manchez?*

A shiver rung his spine, cold and foreboding, and he looked away from the wraith of his long dead partner shaken. "What? No, I don't think so... Do we know each other?" Desmond was certainly fearing the response – that he knew was coming.

"It's alright. I understand. It's been many years, after all, since you killed my father. I've grown a lot. Huh Old man?" Oscar felt the rush of triumph and adrenaline, which comes probably to all professional athletes taking the biggest game of their lives. This was his super bowl ring, his triple crown, his vengeance. Finally served cold, on a perfectly stormy night.

"*Who are you?*" Conway probes, feeling pretty *scrooged* at the moment, having what appeared to be the phantom of a man he'd once killed, now holding a gun to his head.

"I don't always remember the faces of everyone I've *haunted* either... *Naw* - It's just easier to try to forget them, "*Right Desmond?*" Oscar said from his firm position of dominance, with the gun still firmly held towards his cranium. "But the truth is, whether ghosts exist, karma is or is not? One thing is truer than anything – they will haunt us all. *For fucking-ever.* So you can consider me your *mother-fucking reaper* – right bitch? *'Cause I'm the devil come to take your ass to hell."*

Conway began to regret his depraved life, and knew his only hope was trying to bluff his way out, "What are you talking about? I've never killed any-"

"You know - *sure as hell* what I'm talking about Desmond!" Oscar wasn't going to play any games, not with this asshole, and he didn't have the time for it. *"The ghosts of your drunken ass's past; come back to bite!"*

Conway did not like that he knew his real name, a name he'd not heard spoken in years aloud. "What? Look, I've got *kids,* and a *wife,* and-"

"Shut the fuck up! I don't wanna hear it! *My father had kids too...* So don't tell me about it, cause I *really* don't care!"

Conway Pleaded to him from a shivering place, where he felt the warmth of urine fleeing his stressed bladder uncontrollably, *"Okay calm down we all-"*

"Still talking?" Oscar wagged his gun toward Conway.

Conway shut up.

"Now, are you thinking 'bout it?" Oscar asks him.

"Yes..." Conway, suddenly unsure of what he was supposed to be thinking about, was currently reflecting how nice and warm his crotch felt, ironically. "Uh -thinking about what?"

"How we know each other asshole." Oscar never really saw the conversation going so awkwardly as it was now. "You see *all that gold*

and *cash* - just lying there on the ground?"

"Of course I see it. It's mine - *so what?*" Conway was agitated by his lack of options and where the conversation was headed.

Oscar smacked him with a nugget of truth, "*We both know how you got it.*"

Conway finally had a glimmer in his eyes of recognition that he was now hauntingly willing to admit, "*Mm-Manchez?*"

"*That's right...*" Said Oscar - Happy the old crow is finally remembering.

"*Oh my god* - Oscar, is that really you?" Conway's voice *quivered.*

"In the flesh - *Desmond...*" Oscar replied.

"I haven't seen you in what — twenty years?" Conway tried to remember the last time they'd seen each other. *It had been at his Birthday party perhaps?*

"I'm not here to catch up." Oscar was not in the mood for small talk.

"Listen, I know what you must think, but I didn't kill your father." Conway was trying to think of a good story to tell the kid, who was now a full-grown man — with a gun.

"You really think I'm gonna believe anything you've got to say, old man? Come on, you know my daddy didn't raise no fool," Oscar calmly told him.

"No - I guess not." Conway began to break a sweat, as he ran through a very short list of options open to him now.

Option A: *Fight.* Or, option B: *Die.* Was the list he could come up with.

"I can't believe you just happened to show up - as I was stealing back what you stole from my father... Must be *Karma* or something. You have no Idea how glad I am that you are here for this... It's so fitting." Oscar gripped the gun harder. "Now turn around, you miserable bastard, and look at the face of *vengeance.*"

Conway began to cry and weep, hesitating to do as asked, "What! No! Please don't-"

"Turn the fuck around now!" Oscar Barked at him, impatient.

"Don't kill me, please..." What else could Conway say?

Oscar didn't care; his look was cold and ready to sting, he stepped forward and put the cold steel of the gun's barrel to the back of Conway's head to show him he was serious.

Conway was fearful, and suddenly his much more dreadfully sober face had a glimmer of an idea. *"Just take the money. There's no need for this,"* he told Oscar as he prepared to take the only decision open to him - Option A: *Fight.*

Oscar laughed at Conway suggesting he take what he already pretty much had. "That's exactly what I was doing right before you showed up; taking the money. And there is most certainly a need for this; it's called vengeance and survival. But I'm guessing you know what I mean? Being the snake you are."

"Listen Oscar, you don't wanna do this, trust me." Conway was itching for his moment, hoping that he was rushed with enough adrenaline already to follow through with taking on a younger man in battle.

"Trust me, Yes I do wanna-"

At this moment, a rack of wine bottles decided to topple from its awkward position, having been knocked off kilter after the explosion that blew the safe open.

The sudden loud crashing of wine bottles startled Oscar, and he turned his head to scope it out to be sure it was not an unknown threat.

Conway took advantage of the opportunity; he knew it was now or never.

Like the lightning still careening in the sky outside, he suddenly stepped back from where he was standing, slipping his head around and away from the gun very smoothly, as he'd been trained to years before. Conway managed to grab onto Oscar's wrist. With both his hands, he viced his grip upon the gun, trying to wrestle it from him.

Oscar, who was still behind him, and now had his hand holding the gun being attacked, was taken aback by the sudden reverse assault from Conway as their death-lock struggle for control over the handgun became quickly manic, and the two men madly wrestled for dominance over the firepower.

Oscar used Conway's shirt with his free hand to try to choke him back, trying to free himself. Conway, using the grip on Oscar's arm holding the gun, responded to the strangling by lifting him up off his feet and lurching forward, taking Oscar onto his back. He then with all his weight and might lunged suddenly backwards, and Conway Slammed Oscar's Body into the wall behind them hard.

Dust scattered from the already tattered and bombed out walls, as sheetrocking crumbled over them both in a crinkling rain of soot and rock.

Oscar had the wind blown out of him, as Conway had him sandwiched against the wall by the sudden fight for survival.

Oscar's hand was knocked into the edge of a filing cabinet, the piercing pain finally caused him to release his grip upon the gun, and it went falling to the floor. Where it proceeded to be kicked by Oscar's flailing and kicking feet, and the firearm slid twirling out the door of the office and over near the beer coolers fifteen feet away.

Conway jabbed his elbow into Oscar's rib cage and then released his hold on his wrist.

Oscar went falling to the ground, gasping for air, yet still madly focused. He quickly reached out and grabbed Conway's left ankle as he began to dart toward the gun and through the doorway, tripping him up.

Conway went crashing down with a large resounding 'thump.' Dust clouds rose in an odd onion-ring shape around him.

Both of them took a moment to catch their breath, as the powdered air only made them cough, gasping for oxygen.

Oscar peered at Conway with an evil eye, whose coughing through clouds of sheetrock and soot kept his eyes on the prize, getting ready to make his move on the gun again.

Both having restocked their lungs sufficiently enough, and after a tense moment of glaring each other down, Conway was the first to spring into action. Pushing himself up from the floor, he began to sprint out the doorway and into the store's main lobby after the gun, not waiting for his opponent to get there first.

Oscar, with a younger man's vigor, quickly made up for Conway's slight head start, and pounced upon Conway's back with all the venom of years of pent up rage. They met each other once more for a duel over control of the gun lying on the floor by the cooler, in a puddle of beer and shattered glass.

The two foes were interlocked, rolling around the floor, shreds of bottle-glass stabbing into their bodies and cans of food raining down on them from the display shelves. Conway's nails went ripping into Oscar's face, as they clawed skin away in bloody red tears as he attempted to gouge-out Oscar's eyes.

The two competitors were in that moment animals in every sense of the word, both struggling for survival and dominance.

And there could only be one who victor.

"I'm a fucking GhostWalker come to reap your ass!" was the last thing Oscar said to Desmond - before the gun went off.

* 5 minutes previous, 5 miles away
3:05 A.M.

Thunder and lightning flashed and boomed in the sky above as *Officer Peter 'Tate' O'Brien* made his way drunk-driving through the rain-drenched roads very fast towards Conway's Gas Depot.

He had been off duty at the time, and normally would have been sleeping at such an hour - except that he and his wife had had a fight that night over their finances. So like most nights that she had a cold shoulder to him and didn't have to work the next day, he found himself up late moping and drinking beers in the garage with the dogs, listening to old Tony Bennet records.

It was a habit of Tate's to scan the radio, and monitor the chatter from the boys on duty, who were at that moment talking it up about the list of usual suspects for the party ruckus down at the 'ol'watering hole' swim spot.

Officer O'Brien had been reminiscing on how he'd caused much ruckus himself back in the sixties, when the call came in that Conway's store had been *'blown to hell,'* as Kim, the local night shift Police Dispatcher, said Carl had described it.

Tate O'Brien had been briskly drawn away from thoughtful meanderings if his past, and jumped on the opportunity to be the first responder to the emergency. Normally, he would not drink and drive, but knew that it would be a good 40 minutes or so before the only on duty officers would be able to respond to the scene, and being just a few minutes away, found that duty called.

Drunk or not, he wasn't going to miss this show. *It's not every day that Conway's Quikee gas depot blows up, after all.* He'd even brought his new cell phone with video recording capabilities to take footage that he could then sell to the local news.

When Officer O'Brien approached the store, he saw that it *had* been blown from the inside out. He quickly exited his Ford Taurus, into the barrage of rain falling from the sky. He looked around for any signs of life, but could see only Conway's truck parked with a door lodged in it's windshield - but no sign of the man himself.

"Carl!" Tate called out.

Above, flashes and crashes rhymed in the sky, and the sound of thunderous rain droned out the sound of the two men struggling with each other for control of the gun inside.

Suddenly the gun went off.

Tate O'Brien in his drunken state of mind thought the gunshot was thunder; and seeing the flash of light spark from the gun inside the store, he figured that it was probably just an electrical wire shorting out. Not aware of the deadly danger lurking inside, he began to make his way towards the front door, but found it locked.

Grabbing his cell phone from his pocket, and turning the Camera app on to record, Officer Tate then made his way over towards the hole where the window once had been and peered inside. "Unreal," he said as he began to capture the images and sounds of the destruction. Moving in for a closer inspection while pulling out his Mag-Lite to see the carnage better, he noticed a body lying on the floor inside.

"Oh no." He recognized the jeans and sneakers and coat to be Carl Conway's, and saw the pool of blood soaking onto the floor around him, his brains splattered all over the beer coolers, and his legs twitching their last reactionary movements as he quickly died.

"What the fuck happened here?" Tate asked drunkenly to the camera phone.

"Bad timing is what," said Oscar from the smoke filled shadows of the store with his gun pointed toward Tate.

The last view Tate got was of a man, who looked like he'd walked out of a horror film, his face all smudged with ash and marked by Conway's fingernails where they had scratched him up like a wolverine in the struggle.

Oscar then fired a bullet into Tate O'Brien's head, having no concern to dilly-dally with hostages. He then wasted no time and got to work on quickly loading the several dozen gold bars and the cash and diamonds into his car. Unaware that Tate's smartphone was recording *everything*.

Right before getting in the vehicle and fleeing the crime scene, Oscar stopped and turned back to get one last look at Conway's decimated world; a sense of accomplishment welling inside him, "Rest in peace, Pops..." he said aloud to the stormy weather, while checking his army issue watch to see the time.

3:13 A.M.

Jackson and Sheri were perched on a rock together with their eyes closed, as if trying to relax, while Rowan and Vang sat almost similar in pose not far away from them; but nowhere near as intimate or at ease as their captors seemed.

Sheri opened her eyes and looked at Vang and Rowan, who were sitting together overlooking the ocean, as the thunderstorms rolled in across the horizon.

"You two make a beautiful couple. Do you know that?" Sheri remarked to them. Then she got up very calmly and walked towards Rowan and Vang, with a sincere smile, laced with charm. "I mean it. I can see things in people sometimes, and this is one of those times. You two are bound together in some soulful way, I can tell."

"Yeah, we're both *bound* as your hostages..." Vang responded.

Sheri was not very happy that Vang was giving her lip. *"Really?* You're gonna be like that? Still? I was just complimenting you is all." Sheri took a deep breath and tried to calm herself down. "Look, we're being 100% fucking real with you. So, drop the attitude and work with us. *Okay?"*

"Alright, I'm working, just relax..." Vang realized he needed to tone his outrage down.

Jackson interjected, "We were *relaxed* until you gave us shit."

Knowing Jackson's temper and tone, Sheri changed the subject: "Hey-say have you ever heard the joke of the Muppet who walked into a bar of mimes?"

"I like jokes." Rowan agreed with this change of conversation.

"So this Muppet walks in and asks the bartender if he's got any-"

Suddenly Jackson's phone began ringing.

The ring-tone was a song of foreboding to Jackson and Sheri's ears; they all froze what they were doing, and nervousness tinged the moment.

"Give me a second," said Jackson as he turned away from them and checked the message that was sent to his phone. Oscar had sent him a picture text; it was just a picture of a *Seashell*. He was not very happy to see the Seashell. "Oh man..."

"What now?" Sheri perked up to attention, alarmed to see the Seashell. Seashells were bad, *very bad*.

Jackson turned to Sheri with a concerned brow, and only said, "I gotta go..."

"What?!" Sheri was not hip to the idea of splitting up.

Jackson gave her his gun - she reluctantly took it. "You stay here; I'll be back soon." He then kissed her and began to move toward his car.

"What's going on?" Sheri asked him as he went; Jackson pondered his answer, as he pulled a second gun from his pants.

"I don't know..." he replied as he got into the driver's seat, then looking over at her before shutting the door, "Whatever it is; it's not good. I will be back soon though... Okay?"

"Be safe..." she called out to him as he quickly peeled off and away. Sheri turned and looked at Rowan and Vang with fear in her eyes, mixed with concern, as Jackson sped off to meet Oscar.

Sheri was worried; the plan had been deviated from, which was a foreboding sign to her.

Vang took this moment to appeal to Sheri. "Please, just let us go, we have nothing to do with whatever is going on with you two."

Sheri put her gun-less hand to her brow as if a headache were coming on, "Look, I have tried to explain to you that we *really are* helping you; you got to trust me on this."

Rowan demanded to know, "How is holding us hostage helping us?"

Sheri tried to find the right way to tell her. "Because it sure as hell is better than the alternative."

Rowan felt a lightness flush her cheeks and ripple through her chest. "I'm guessing we wouldn't like the alternative..."

"No you wouldn't." Sheri was finding that Altruism was not so easy in practice.

Rowan decided it was time to state the obvious. "This is *really* messed up."

Sheri was torn up that her new friend, the girl she was trying to save, was now terrified of her. She wanted to explain to Rowan that she had the best intentions for her. Sheri had just finished reading a book about Altruism the week before Oscar showed up trying to enlist Jackson's help in his heist scheme. After hearing the story of Oscar's father, she and Jackson agreed to help, on one condition: *that no one got hurt.*

"Awe man... You guys, it's tearing me up that you think I'm just some *crazy bitch with a gun* and a loose cannon boyfriend...

"Well kind'a – yeah..." She was meditating on the way of *Lion Tamer, No fear...*

"Yeah, I agree that's a fair assessment of how we feel," Vang agreed with both of them.

"You're not making us feel very warm and

fuzzy inside, you know..." Rowan said this with an earnest concern for the woman, and themselves, using a consoling tone.

Sheri looked up to both of them with a wincing guilt. *"You see.* Awe... Look – it's like this; your boss Conway has a *history*. And it isn't good, and tonight – well tonight is the night he gets what's coming to him..."

"What does her boss have to do with us?" Vang wondered aloud.

Sheri shuffled, not used to the weight of a gun in her hand, "Right now; a lot..."

Rowan was trying to think of what this could be about, but really couldn't pinpoint anything in particular off the top of her head. "I'm not following your logic here? I have very little to do with Conway."

Sheri "You know that safe in the backroom of his?"

"Yeah."

"What do you think is *really* in there?"

Rowan was pretty flabbergasted that they did all this for a measly little drop box safe. "Knowing Conway? Probably just a few thousand dollars, maybe a gun or two and his business papers."

"Naw, he's fucking loaded. He's got a huge hidden wall safe as well. You see, before he settled down and bought that shit-hole that you work at-" Sheri suddenly realized that her choice of words might have been condescending to Rowan, seeing that she worked there. "No offense, Honey."

"If it quacks like a duck." Rowan agreed with her statement.

"Well anyway he was a death dealer."

Rowan was not sure what that meant. "He was a what?"

"You know, a black market weapons dealer; he sold tons of stuff to all sorts of shady people around the world. Get it? And he killed people, and provided the munitions to kill many people too..." Sheri let this little nugget of information sink in for a moment.

Rowan was trying to imagine Conway as an evil James Bond type person, trotting the globe and buddying-it-up with dictators as a mercenary.

But this vision was fuzzy.

"Are you sure you have the right guy? I mean - Carl? I mean he's a real sleaze ball, yes - but really? Really, Carl?"

"100% Positive." Sheri had seen the files.

Vang's critical thinking set in, and his mouth soon followed. "The Tsunami story was bogus. So how do we know that you're not just lying to us again?"

Sheri didn't like all the questions. "*That bogus story* is what saved your damned life, Sweetie. I came up with it myself, to save my boyfriend's buddy from killing you."

Rowan was shocked, stunned, floored, and slapped in the face all in one by this sudden and terrifying revelation.

"He's a real nut, this guy, the kind that should probably not be walking around with a gun; *know what I mean?*" Sheri added as she waved the pistol in her hand as if it were a cigarette. "And that just would not have been right... I mean you shouldn't have to die for another man's crimes."

Sheri, emotionally, yet sternly made clear, "So please, look at me, and my man, - as your guardian angels, who wouldn't let harm come to you."

Vang and Rowan were stupefied by the turn of events in her confession.

Vang was speechless, but Rowan managed to mumble, "That is a pretty wild story..."

Vang found a shining light in the darkness of the situation. "So then you're saying that you're like Bonnie; and your boyfriend is like Clyde - doing some Robin-Hood shit or something?"

Sheri smiled at the way Vang put it. "Yeah, I guess we are kind like that, sure..." Then she remembered how the movie ended. "Wait, didn't they both die at the end of that movie?"

3:19 A.M.

Jackson parked his car next to Oscar's on the side of the road, near the *bear totem pole,* and he got out to meet him in the pouring rain between the two cars. He instantly saw that his face was all scratched up; blood seeped from the fresh wounds mixing with the water trickling down his skin in rivers.

"What the hell happened to you?" Jackson did not like the looks of things.

Oscar stared him cold in the eye. "Desmond happened. Of all my dumb luck, the rat bastard was driving by right when I blew the safe, bro'."

"You blew the safe?!" Jackson began to feel very frustrated.

"I had to; the bastard had changed the combination to the safe."

"So what happened?" Jackson knew what had happened.

"What do you think happened? I capped his ass." Oscar said it unapologetically.

"Oscar, no one was supposed to get hurt!" Jackson knew this complicated matters *immensely.*

"What do you want from me? It happened. So what? Motherfucker had it coming anyway, so let's soldier on bro, I got the loot - we won." He slapped him on the shoulder and gave him a bloody smirk.

"Anything else happen that wasn't a part of the plan?" Jackson hoped that was all, but he could tell by the look on Oscar's face that there was more bad news coming.

"There was this guy who showed up; I had to kill him too, and he ended up being a cop." Oscar knew that was not what he wanted to hear, but better now than never, he figured.

"What!" Jackson began to feel panic grab him by the balls. "Oh, man, we're fucked! You have totally screwed us all, Oscar."

"After all we've been through overseas, you're gonna hold this against me now? Right after I scored us a fortune? Instead of being sent home to unemployment hell? I scored for us heavy, *bro'*. You should be thanking me that I'm even sharing this score with you..."

Jackson looked at Oscar absurdly. "Sure... We're rich... But you left one large mess back there, Oscar! The plan was that the money was dirty and untraceable, so the cops wouldn't be looking for us very hard." Jackson pointed towards his face. "Look at you. You probably left a trail of evidence, and a *dead cop* back there!"

Oscar didn't care to defend his actions any further. "It'll be all good, so just chill the fuck out."

"Chill?! How? We're gonna see a man hunt for our asses, cause you fucking killed a cop! This shit's whacked!" Jackson was very much disturbed by Oscar's casual demeanor over the issue.

"Relax; everything will be fine, once we tie up a few of these loose ends." Oscar was certain it must be done now.

Jackson put his foot down in a puddle; it splashed mud upon Oscar's ash-laden jeans. "We are not killing them."

"Them?" Oscar was only aware of the girl Rowan.

"This kid she knew showed up, and things got complicated." Jackson began to feel a sickness in his stomach.

"Really? You're the ones they can recognize, bro'. You and your bitch are the-"

Jackson snapped and slapped Oscar upside the head hard and quick. "What did I say about calling her that?!"

Oscar gave him the hit without a push back; instead, he sneered at him, "You and your honey are the ones the cops are gonna be looking for. I'm sure they will be more than willing to tell them all about you guys, describe your features and everything..." Oscar appealed to the warrior in Jackson. "Are you really gonna put yourself willingly through all that? For some people you don't even know?"

Jackson knew it was a cluster of a situation. "Fuck!" he screamed to the sky.

Oscar chuckled, "Now you think about that while you help me unload the gold and loot into your car. We ain't got much time left before the hounds'll be sniffing our trail."

Jackson took a deep breath, trying to calm the fear boiling inside him.

Oscar could tell Jackson's emotions were brewing; he opened the door to his car to begin unloading the cargo. "So, are you still with me; or are you against me?"

Jackson's fists were clenching air hard as he thought it over, not liking any of his options. "Sheri is not gonna like this..."

"Sheri's just along for the ride; who cares what she thinks?" Certainly not Oscar.

"If you haven't noticed? I care. I love her man..."

"*That's cool...* I'm sure if she really loves you too, you'll work it out. Right?" Oscar looks him in the eye to see if he's on board with the plan still, or if he's over board.

Jackson knew Oscar was summing up his resolve. "Yeah--right..."

Oscar checked his watch to see that it was 3:23 A.M. "We gotta get this show on the road *now.*"

Jackson knew they must get moving, and began to help Oscar unload the loot from the car as fast as he could. When they were done, Oscar took a large red fuel canister from the back of his car and proceeded to pour the gasoline into the interior. He then pushed the cigarette lighter in and waited a few seconds. When it popped up hot and ready, he took it and tossed it onto the fuel soaked upholstery, setting the car ablaze. It went up like a mushroom clouded bonfire, and lashed out at the pouring rain with its hissing flames and dark smoke.

Oscar, content that he destroyed it sufficiently, not there to watch it burn, then got into Jackson's Subaru and turned to his oldest companion with a smile from his scarred and bleeding face.

It was a wild smile of a man on the edge.

"*No pain, no gain.*" Said Oscar. "Now let's get this shit *done...*"

Jackson put the car into gear and headed back towards Perkins Pier, a deep sorrow heavy on his brow, and a huge decision rifting his heart, soul, and mind.

He was being torn, having to choose between Love and Loyalty.

3:25 A.M.

"So what's your story, anyway? What brought a kid like you out here to the middle of nowhere this late at night? For real, this time too, and not just another bullshit story like the last one."

"I'm taking the long way home." Vang cracked a wise-guy smile and quickly noticed that Sheri wasn't digging it. "Well, I'm headed home from college and I like driving at night; it's just usually a calmer drive at night, and when I saw that Rowan might be in trouble, well I just wanted to make sure that she was – okay. So I followed you here to be sure."

Sheri's face lit up with excitement. "That's so – *Altruistic*..."

"Sure – I guess." Vang did not completely understand what she meant, but isn't going to disagree either, having seen how uptight she'd gotten with all the questions earlier.

Rowan took this moment to admire Vang's chivalrous nature. "You got yourself mixed up in this - to try and help me?"

Vang shyly looked Rowan in her youthfully glowing eyes and nervously smiled back. "Yeah. I mean I wasn't stalking you or anything. I was just concerned is all."

"Oh my god *it's a sign;* you're a servant of altruistic energies... You're like her fucking guardian angel in the living flesh."

"Whatever." Vang anxiously felt that she was about to go back to *Crazy-Land* again.

Sheri clarified, "There was this man once; his name was *George Price,* and he was like this genius mathematician back in the day who worked on the *Manhattan Project* – you know

143

with the *Atomic Bomb* and all - as well as all sorts of other very important things in his life-time." She was trying to find the quickest way to *make her point* for them as she took a ponderous pause. Not wanting to tangent, she once again focused on *"The Main Point being* this guy got *very wealthy* from his endeavors. But then he one day had this - *Vision*. Maybe he was on drugs, maybe it was just a funny dream, maybe he was crazy; who knows? *The point* being; that he *honestly believed* that *God* had chosen *him* to mathematically prove that Altruism really existed among complete strangers. He spent the rest of his life trying to spread *True Kindness;* he went on *a mission* to *prove* that kindness wasn't *just a genetic trait* which we only share with our family and ethnicities..."

Vang was intrigued, but skittish about how it related to him. "That's fascinating... But what's it got to do with me?"

"Well - right now you're the miracle of Altruism in action, and you're validating my attempt to partake in the *Miracle* of it as well."

"Okay?" Still stretching his logic, he was having trouble computing what kind of *'Altruistic kindness'* could be drawn from being threatened with a gun and held hostage in the middle of the night, but decided her tangents were way better than being threatened and screamed at, so he mused to her, "So what happened to this guy?"

"Well - he kinda' went destitute trying to save the poor from their lot; then became a vagabond - before finally killing himself with a pair of scissors..."

"Huh." Rowan was not sure what to make of the ending to the story Sheri had just shared with them about this Altruistic man, who had supposedly been chosen by god to save the humanity from itself, ironically after helping create one of the scariest and most threatening weapons the world's ever seen, too?

Must be true Rowan thought to herself. *Who would write such a miserable ending to a story?*

Real Life; that's who...

Rowan and Vang at this moment both shared a collective fear - that this unstable and strange couple was threatening to write a horrendous ending to their own personal biographies. Yet somehow Sheri's talk of kindness was like a *Silver Lining* of possibility, they both desperately hoped that *it really would be okay.*

The two of them stood together, almost as if silently in prayer, yearning to have the opportunity to survive this night, so that they would have an opportunity to continue to breathe and play among the world's living for a little longer, and be given the ability to write their own *destiny's* ending.

Sheri noticed that their minds were seizing up on what she'd said; she could tell they thought she was crazy. She *needed* them to understand that she really was *trying to be kind*, so Sheri said to them, trying to snap them to epiphany, "But what's *important* is that he *really believed* in it, he saw it in the world and tried to spread it around. He helped many people in his time. He wanted to prove that we don't need to be genetically related to be honestly kind to others. And, well, you and I – we, are living proof of that..."

Vang quickly changed the subject away from his altruism. "If that's so true, then how come we're your hostages? That's the part that really confuses me."

Sheri didn't like the logic-fork in the road of her Altruism kick. "Things get complicated outside of theory; the world throws stuff at you that tests our limits sometimes. But my intentions are pure; *please just trust me.*"

"*Trust?* Show us some trust and just let us go right now." Rowan had never done hostage negotiation before this evening. She needed to take charge, and didn't want to give her fears any energy - so she focused on the positive with Sheri, and asked her, "Prove to us your Altruistic intentions and *Trust us* by letting us go free right now."

Sheri so wished that was the way it could be, but knew that it wasn't, not yet anyway. "I will – soon enough. But for right now, you just need to just chill with me, until Jackson returns."

Rowan was trying to think of what else she could say to convince her not to go all Charles Manson on them, but only found "But *why?*" exiting her mouth.

"*Because* that's just the way it has to be. So enough with the why's already! I'm sorry; but you stay here with me until the job's over. Now drink your damned beer and be grateful that I'm such a nice *bitch!...*"

Vang and Rowan turned to each other, mirroring irony in their pose; Rowan broke it with a smile. "You know, she's right."

"About what?" he asked.

"You *are* very sweet for trying to make sure I was okay. You weren't very *good at it*; but it *was* very brave of you," she commended him.

Sheri felt the fluid interaction that Vang and Rowan shared in their mood together, and wondered, "How long have you two known each other?"

"We really just met tonight, actually. So I guess just two hours or so," Vang tallied.

Sheri jumped up, excited, and giggled as if she'd just won the lottery. "Oh my god, you guys have got *the Spark.*" Sheri had felt it with Jackson; that's how she recognized it in them. "The match that lights the freakin' fires of love is bright between you two. I have an eye for these things..."

Sheri said this so matter-of-factly; awkward shuffles danced at Rowan and Vang's shy feet. With darting eyes, they were both glad the dim light hid their simultaneous blushing.

"You two are gonna have a bright future together, I can tell." Sheri then wondered, "Oh, what Zodiacal signs are you guys, by the way?" Sheri didn't really know that much about the *Science,* or *MoJo,* or *whatever* was behind the *Star Signs;* but loved finding out the answers nonetheless.

Rowan looked up to the sky, stormy clouds quickly moving and swirling above her - surfing on the winds turbulence.

Like facts, swimming and swirling around the vortex of our minds.

Rowan thought about Paradigm Shifts, and the thirteenth Zodiacal Sign, while watching lightning crawl across the horizon like electric lizards, and it suddenly struck her, the thought.

There is only one constant in life; things Always change, for better or worse. The one sure thing that you could depend on was that things

will always be changing.
Rearranging, morphing, and swirling.
Just like this moment now.

Rowan knew that even facts had a way of changing, or being proven wrong, eventually anyways – if given enough time and perspective, that is. "I'm not sure anymore; they say that we have *13 Zodiacal Signs* now, and the calculations are being updated to represent the world's constellational alignments to today's placements in the galaxy right now, and not the alignment of the earth and stars as it was 2,000 years ago."

"Really? A Thirteenth-Zodiacal Sign? That's weird; where has the thirteenth been hiding all this time?" Sheri had not heard of this. Oddly enough, it wasn't in her daily horoscope in the paper that morning.

"It actually makes sense. There are thirteen full moons in a year, though there really isn't a universally accepted unit of time for calculating a year. We go by the Gregorian calendar the Chinese the Lunar calendar, and so forth." Rowan stated thoughtfully. "It can get confusing, but on average it as about twenty-nine days, twelve hours and forty-four minutes between each moon."

"Oh girl you *definitely* need to go back to College." Sheri was amazed at the depth of knowledge Rowan had at her disposal about the sky above, which still at the moment rampaged the chaos of nature's full fury upon them; rain sprayed their faces again in the turbulent winds.

Sheri turned to her wandering concern for Jackson, and after a moment of suspenseful waiting silence, she finally saw the signs of car headlights entering the park.

They all watched with a pounding heartbeat and a held breath, as the vehicle approached.

Sheri found her itching and slippery hand gripping the gun tighter, until she was positive that it was Jackson.

To her relief - and Vang and Rowan's bemoaned anticipation - they saw, finally, that in fact it was Jackson returning.

After parking the car, he slowly, almost mournfully exited the Subaru, and began to walk over toward her, stopping halfway he then waved for Sheri to join him, away from Rowan and Vang's earshot.

"Don't you go anywhere; we'll be right back..." Jackson said, pointing to them with his finger sticking out from a fisted hand.

He didn't even wait for them to respond, and quickly grabbing Sheri's arm, he almost tugged her away from them.

Sheri was glad to see Jackson, yet she knew the look on his face was of concern. "What's happened?"

He did not want to say what he had to say to her. "Things -- went bad..."

"What? You didn't get the money? After all this?" She tossed her hands up in the air, disheveled.

"No-no. We got the money... But things went bad none the less..."

"Oh no. Where's Oscar? Is he okay?" Sheri looked toward the car's interior, and saw Oscar's hazy shadow through the rain splotched glass and the beaming headlights of the car.

Jackson grabbed her arm again to snap her back to what he had to say. "Oscar's fine; he's in the car– but right now, we've got other fish to fry."

"Well, then, spit it out. What happened?"

Jackson gave in. "Oscar killed him... Them."

Sheri was mortified. "What? Killed *who?*"

Jackson winces. "Desmond... and a cop, too..."

Sheri did not want to believe what she'd just heard him say, but Jackson wouldn't say it if it weren't true. "Awe fuck! Shit, Jackson, how'd this happen?! No one was supposed to be there!"

Jackson, having had no control, didn't want to hear it from her. "Yeah, well, they were, and Oscar – reacted... And well, now *we're* the main suspects in their murder - once *they* I.D. *us* that is..."

Sheri looked over at Rowan and Vang sitting together over by the rock, in the misting rain, nervously watching them talk excitedly.

They could tell something bad had happened, as worry was thick in the air like fog.

"*Oh no... We're not gonna?!*" She knew the way Oscar thought. "*No!*"

"I'm not sure we have many good options on the table right now, Sheri." He didn't like it any better than she did, but was at a loss as to what could be done.

Sheri looked over sorrowfully at Vang and Rowan. She liked these kids, and knew they did not deserve such a fate. "We're gonna leave them right here. Let's go, *right now.* I can't do this. I won't do this!" She began to push Jackson back towards the car, not having any part of it.

Vang, sensing that things were getting wildly unhinged and dangerous again, quickly whispered into Rowan's ear. "This might be a good time to run."

Rowan hesitated in doing this. "That might just provoke something worse."

Oscar, watching as Sheri pushed Jackson towards the car - trying to stop the inevitable, was losing his patience, he decided that if Sheri and Jackson couldn't agree to get it done.

Well then, he must.

Getting out of the car, his face all freshly scarred up and a determined look on it, Oscar began to move toward Vang and Rowan to do the job himself, calling out to Jackson as he went towards them, "We don't have the time for this catty bullshit, bro! We gotta go *now!*"

Jackson was torn between his friend's need - and what he knew was *wrong*.

Vang and Rowan were alarmed by the sudden and hostile approach of Oscar, an unknown and unseen person up until now. His wounds made him appear ghoulish in a real life nightmare manifest before them.

"You mean provoke something like this?" Vang said to Rowan, his voice tense with doom, as Oscar began to pull his gun from the belt-line of his pants.

Rowan was ready to stop procrastinating. "Yeah, I think it's definitely time to run." They both then began their escape away from Oscar, who was closing in on them fast and furious.

Sheri, realizing this was happening, turned to Jackson for support, yet found him frozen, just standing there watching Oscar get closer to them. "Stop him," she screamed.

Jackson, turning back to her, "What do you want me to say to him? You don't know how he is. I've never been able to stop him from doing anything – *ever.*"

Oscar got ever closer to them, aiming his gun to shoot Vang and Rowan in cold blood. Vang cried out to the assailant, scared, "Hey-hey, We got no beef with you, there is no need for this."

"We haven't ever done anything to you..." added Rowan, in hopes it would stop him somehow.

Oscar cackled a cold hiss. "Yeah, and you'll never *have the chance* either..." Oscar, with his gun pointing toward Rowan, pulled the trigger heartlessly.

Eight shots were fired rapidly from his gun towards them. And to his astonishment, a sudden gust of wind set every single one of them astray from their target.

Vang realized it was time to act quicker; he grabbed Rowan's arm and pulled her behind him as Oscar fired another shot that missed them, as they continued struggling to get away from lunatic trying to kill them. As he got closer to them, aiming his gun at them once more, Oscar fired another bullet.

Vang using his body to shield Rowan from the assailant, managed to find himself the target. His arm spewed a small flesh-wound splatter of blood as he took a bullet and released a bellow of pain from his mouth. His feet stumbling on a wet rock, he slipped to the ground.

Oscar used the moment to catch up to them, as Rowan struggled to help Vang back onto his feet. Coming to a stop, the reaper aimed his gun towards Rowan and Vang, pulling the trigger again.

But lucky for them, the clip was empty.

Rowan was thrown into tears as the moment of her death had been shortly postponed.

Once more.

Vang, who was gasping for air while wincing from the pain of being shot, was lying in a mud puddle that was sprouting hundreds of tiny splattering ripples from the falling raindrops.

Rowan tried to pull him up from the ground. Using his good arm, she gave him her hand, and they tugged each other into a sprint toward the cliff outreach in the park, towards the *Lighthouse* weathering the storm lashing the shore.

Oscar began closing in on them again, fast, charging with his gun pointed, ready to strike like the *Viper he was*. When he had finally caught up with them and they had no where else to run, used the moment to catch his breathe from the dash, lightheaded from the loss of blood, pulling out a fresh clip he began to reload his gun, but before he could finish -

A shot was fired.

Oscar's shirt began to bleed, trickling blood from the wound ripped through his chest. He just stood there for a moment, in shock, as the person who shot him from behind walked around his side and became visible to him.

Sheri was standing there with a smoking gun in her hands, having just done the deed from ten feet back. She too was almost as much in shock at having shot Oscar as he was at having been shot.

"I told you we were not gonna kill anyone, especially no one innocent..." she said to him, as tears began welling in her eyes. Jackson arriving late on the scene took the gun from Sheri's hand. She looked at the man she loved; remorse was in her – with tears flowing from her eyes.

Jackson then walked over to his dying friend, who was still standing, stunned, an expression of disbelief upon his face, a fresh bullet clip in one hand, and his gun in the other, looking at Jackson, perplexed.

"You gave -- that crazy bitch a gun *um'bray*?" Blood was now working its way out his mouth from his interior bleeding. "What the hell were you thinking?"

Oscar felt his wound draining his life force quickly, and it finally hit him – the mortality of the shot to his chest. Oscar fell to his knees, buckling to the inevitable.

Being the man he was, though, Oscar tried to load the bullet clip into his gun, not wanting to give up.

But Jackson very gently and calmly removed them from his hands, knowing his friend's need to fight to the last moment. Jackson calmly said, "I don't think you'll be doing that again any time soon..." then embraced his brother's hand. " Man, why did you have to be so-- so damned -- Broken?"

Oscar really did not know what to say about that, so he tried to focus on the *Superbowl* moment he'd had with *Desmond*. "We -were so close to winning this time."

Jackson tried to console him. "No man. We made it. *You got the gold and killed that bastard...*"

"Yeah... I did." Oscar knew that he had few words left and chose wisely, finally saying to Jackson with a smile, pleased with himself, "Didn't I say I would get vengeance with him -- even if it killed me?"

"You're a GhostWalker..."

Oscar laughed his last joyful moment and said, "That's right... **'Corruerint Vadit Ad Dura Vita'** –it was Latin for *'a broken man goes to a* *hard life,'* and Jackson knew it was written on Oscar's chest in ink, right near his heart, and now had a bullet hole in it as an exclamation point. They had both gotten the same tattoo when they were the only of the original *'GhostWalkers'* to return from the war the previous year.

Not so proud anymore...

Jackson, "You're gonna be okay. We'll get you to a hospital."

Oscar looked at Jackson with thickly ironic eyebrows and a smile of insane epiphany, "All that -only to be fragged by that crazy bitch in the end?.. *Fuck!..*" *And they were the last words that Oscar ever said.*

The moment was always haunting, one Jackson had seen too often, when life leaves the eyes, the body ceases to be alive. The moment when *'the lights go out'* and all the dreams and hopes of the person go with it into the darkness.

Oscar and Jackson stared at each other in shock and regret, one living - and one dead.

Sheri couldn't watch as he died; she had turned away and was looking out towards the stormy ocean. "I'm sorry..." she said, to everyone without looking at anybody.

Jackson didn't need an apology; he'd rather forget it happened; it was the way soldiers coped.

"It's not your fault; he was such a broken man... And I never had the glue to put him right... You did what you had to do." Jackson said, as Sheri finally faced what she had done and knelt over Oscar's body and looked in his vacant and lifeless eyes, then reaching out her hand she closed them with her fingers as she said a prayer for him.

"Blessed spirits, guardians of our souls, please have mercy on this man... May he rest in peace - *wherever he goes...*" Sheri, suddenly emotionally upset, got mad and slammed her fist on Oscar's dead chest. "You fucking asshole!" she screamed at his corpse angrily. "Why did you have to make me do this?!"

Jackson took her into his arms. "It's okay..."

"*I told them we were their guardian angels, Jackson...*" Sheri sobbed into his shoulder.

Jackson understood what she'd done, and was not really hurt by it, though he was sad that things had come to this.

"It's okay. He needed to be stopped. I'm sorry I froze – I should have been the one doing something to stop him; he'd gone rabid, I know..."

Vang and Rowan were still huddled together, lying on the ground not far from the dead man who almost executed them. They were still in shock from what went down - and what could be next.

The lighthouse, which still towered solid in the distance, despite the pounding of the ocean's furious waves lashing the rocky shoreline, was the only witness to the events.

"Why did you save us?" asked Rowan.

Sheri looked over to her and said nothing for a moment, then blandly, as if tired, responded, "I didn't save you - I saved *us...*" She looked over toward her love, Jackson.

"I guess I did it because I knew our love couldn't survive killing two innocent people in cold blood. – It wasn't true altruism perhaps, but it works."

Jackson stood forth, very serious. "Works? We still have ourselves a few problems here, if you haven't noticed!   Like murder, and witnesses..." he reminded her.

Sheri looked over to Vang and Rowan, then back towards Jackson.   "I just saved them from getting executed. I don't think they would thank us by telling anyone about what happened here that would implicate us."

Vang perked up, wincing with pain from his wounded arm as he moved. "I know we all can live with that."

Rowan agreed, "Damn straight we can." Jackson paced again, then stomped to a halt with a small kick. "Them police are gonna ask you all sorts of questions about tonight, and what do you propose to tell them? Huh?"

Rowan smiled and said, "Simple - *The truth.*"

Jackson was nervous at how she said this. "See, that doesn't work for us-"

Rowan cut him off. "No, Wait, listen. *The truth* about Conway being a shady man, with a dark history, and this man threatening to kill us... Besides that, we know nothing..."

Jackson is listening. "And?"

"And - A man I've never seen before, came in and took me hostage, then left me stranded out here. I then took his gun when he dropped it after slipping on a rock chasing me down, and I shot him - in self defense."

Jackson looked over at Vang, who was wounded. "What about him? He's gonna need to go to a hospital here soon. They're gonna know he was shot, and connect him to these events."

"Again, we go with the truth." She turned to Vang, "That you were brave, and tried to rescue me, but the violent man shot you as we were trying to escape," she said to him warmly.

"That *actually* sounds pretty tight," Vang commented.

Sheri liked the idea. "You and I both know we're not gonna just kill them.... So do we really have any other choice?"

Jackson and Sheri were looking at each other; Jackson was hesitant in wanting to go along with it, but finally deciding what he should do, he moved to complete the task.

Vang and Rowan began to be fearful when Jackson took the gun he'd taken from Oscar and put the fresh bullet clip into it with a hard loud *'Thwack,'* then began to move closer toward them with it held firmly in his hand, aimlessly toward the ground.

Rowan, not liking this man's history with guns, sadly said to him, "So I guess we don't have a deal?"

Jackson pointed his finger at both of them very seriously. "Now, this is one of those really rare moments in life." He frisked his chin whiskers seeking the right words in his head, as he leaned down, peering into their eyes with serious coldness. "Now, I'm not going to threaten you with what happens if you betray us. All I'll say is that it wouldn't be good for any of us, and leave it at that. Now, give me your hands." Jackson said to Rowan.

"What for?" She asked, concerned the answer would not be likable.

"For that story to hold up, you need some gun residue on your hands, so give me your hands and trust me." Jackson put out his palm, waiting for her to do as asked.

Rowan hesitantly reached her hands out and met his. "So what do I do?"

Jackson, using both his hands, put Oscar's Glock-9mm in her hand and helped her fire it once. Then after wiping it clean of any prints tossed the gun to Oscar's feet, splashing it into a mud puddle.

"Now you have scientific implication as well. If you vary from your story – they'll think you're in on it somehow... So shoot your arrow straight with us and them, and all will be okay, alright?" Jackson was trying to read whether they were playing them for fools.

Sheri stood forward, her smile nervous but sincere. "Rowan, I killed a man for you. Do I need to say anything more?"

The two hostages were both ready to agree to whatever got them out alive. Rowan stepped forward. "No, we got it, and I will not forget what you've done for me, for us, and we'll never tell another soul. Really, thank you."

Sheri looked toward the stormy lightning filled horizon, then back toward the two shivering and shell-shocked kids and said, "All this violence stuff - it's not really us."

Jackson stopped pacing and looked at them. "We're trying to do the right thing here; remember that when the police are drilling you."

"We will," said Vang, trying to let him know they were serious about the deal that allowed them to live.

Rowan hugged Sheri; the two were genuine in the moment. "I can't believe I'm giving my kidnapper a sincere hug," she said as they embraced.

"I know, this is so beautifully weird, right?" Sheri agreed. She turned toward Vang and said to him, "You take care of her. Okay?"

Vang found this to be a funny thing to say. "I'm sure she can take care of herself. As for me, I need to get to a hospital, remember, so I think it'll be more like she'll be taking care of me."

Jackson examined the damage and scoffed, "Well, you're going to have to walk. We need the time to get away. That scratch isn't that bad; I've seen way worse - And you'll survive just fine." Jackson threw Vang a handkerchief from his pocket, for the bleeding. "Tie off the wound with that, and just take it easy."

Vang took the handkerchief and looked up to them both. "Thanks, really – for not killing us."

Sheri, wiping tears and rain from her face, said, "I wish things had been different; I bet we could have been good friends."

Rowan, tired yet wholeheartedly, said to them, "You saved our lives; I think that is a good start to a great friendship, if you ask me."

Sheri began to cry at hearing this. "That's so sweet of you to say, really it is. After all we've put you through."

"Maybe Altruism isn't dead after all, huh?" Rowan added.

Sheri laughs, "maybe not."

"I think it's still kicking and screaming..." Rowan said with her classic sarcasm and delightful smile.

Sheri returned the smile, then waved a kiss goodbye as she and Jackson got into their car, and he began dialing the radio for something that pleased him. Finding nothing, he turned it off. Then took a moment to connect with Sheri's eyes, "I sure hope they do what they say. I want to believe there are still good people left in the world..."

"Me too," she agreed.

Jackson then put his foot to the gas and sped off into the night. They drove along the dark road, chasing the shadows of the headlights interacting with the trees. Sheri was looking into the horizon, and watching the storm that was beginning to calm its fury.

"Fucking righteous..." she whispered hauntingly to her love about their escape and massive newfound wealth.

Jackson looked over, not completely hearing what she'd said, his thoughts distracted by the stormy horizon dancing lightning still. "What?"

Sheri looked into his eyes; they shared a moment, leaving Jackson in a place where he didn't need to know what she said, cause it was written on her face, etched in her soul, and clear as day.

She loved him with all her heart.

"Oscar was right about one thing; you *are* one crazy bitch."

Sheri smiled at his wisecrack. "You best be glad that I'm *crazy for you.*"

He was glad.

3:53 A.M.

Rowan took the handkerchief into her hands, from Vang's, as he was ineffectively trying to apply it to his arm to stop the bleeding.

"Here, let me do that." She tied it tightly around his wound, as he winced and gasped in pain. "Oh, I'm sorry..." Rowan, was taken by him; and her eyes spoke it very loudly to him.

He, looking back, was timid.

Rowan took the opportunity that presented itself, she reached over and gently grabbed his neck then pulling him gently toward her lips, she kissed him.

He responded with all the same passion, and when the moment had climaxed, and their lips parted ways, they gazed into each other's *'soul windows'* - awestruck.

"That was – *unexpected*," said Vang, very pleased.

As the moment passed, "Wow..." said Rowan.

"*Wow?* – I'm bleeding to death after helping save you and that's all you have to say?" Vang laughingly goaded her.

"Okay *Wow'zers*. Is that better?"

Vang smiled. "Yeah, that'll work."

Rowan stood up and put her hand out to help him up from where he sat. "Come on, we got a few miles to walk." He took her hand and was lifted up again, and the two of them began walking towards the road. "They stole our phones." Rowan realized suddenly.

"And my car keys, but at least we still have our lives," Vang pointed out.

"This is true." She admitted, as a car came speeding upon them, weaving as it came. When it got closer, she could see that it was Lisa's BMW, and she was still wagoning around with the 'Dumbtourage' of Tony, Scott and 'Tiny'.

Her car stopped in the road and they all get out, a waft of smoke exiting with them. They then proceeded to laugh at Vang and Rowan stranded out here in the pouring rain, soaked and shivering.

"Yo, look what trash the storm blew in," said Tony with his swaggering demeanor, as the other kids laughed at his wisecrack.

"Tony, not right now, we need to get my friend to the hospital – he's been shot," Rowan said to him, not in the mood.

"For real?" Tiny asked her, looking him over. Vang showed them his bloody shirt, and his gimpy and bleeding arm.

"Damn that's ghetto dog. How'd it happen yo?" asked Tony.

"I'll tell you as we go, we just need to get him to a hospital now. Okay?"

Lisa hesitates from letting them into her car. "I don't want him bleeding on my dad's BMW; *he'd kill me,*" she told them pretentiously.

"I'll warp my shirt around him so it soaks it up," Rowan said, trying to limit the potential of damaging the cars upholstery.

"I don't know, maybe we should just call you an ambulance," she said to them. Taking her cell phone from her pocket, it glowed as it was brought from sleep.

"Yo babe, that's some cold shit," Tony said to Lisa. Tony might be a bully, but even he was stunned by her human callousness and lack of concern for his injury, her only interest being about daddy's expensive toy. "If I needed a ride to the hospital, would you leave me cold like that too?"

"Yes, if you're gonna make a mess of everything," she said flatly, and matter of fact.

Suddenly, at this moment the whirring sound of Murdock's beat up old truck could be heard approaching from the access road, and he came hurtling towards Lisa's BMW like a drunken comet, and with no sign of even having applied the brakes, then went crashing into the rear of her precious car parked in the middle of the road.

The sound made was a smashing chorus of materials shattering in unison.

Followed by Lisa's screams of terror.

She watched in horror, and Vang and Rowan in slight karmic joy, as daddy's treasure lay wrecked and torn asunder like tin foil before their eyes. The BMW was pushed forward 15 or 20 feet, and Murdock's truck was wedged into the back of the sedan.

Beer cans were spraying through exploded shells of aluminum as they were scattered randomly throughout the scene of carnage as the collision came to a screeching wrest.

Murdock, not wearing his seatbelt, was knocked unconscious, his head bleeding as he was slumped over the steering wheel. His windshield cracked as beer splatter pissed down on him in a fizz of vehemence.

"My fuuucking caaarrr!" Lisa squealed in rage at seeing it destroyed by Murdock's drunk driving.

A smile came to Vang's face. *If that's not instant karma, then what is,* he thought? He fancied the thought that if this girl had not hesitated to help him, and they had been driving towards the hospital, that perhaps her car would be just fine right now.

Rowan too was thinking very similar thoughts: *how ironic.*

Tony pulled out his cell phone. "Guess that settles it," he said and began dialing 911. Tiny and Scott began to check out the scene of the crash, to see whether Murdock was alive, and they found that yes, in fact he was, as he began to come back to a drunken consciousness, mumbling, *"That wa's's - one big - fucking deer?.."*

Tiny got it all on his video phone, and began laughing as he said to the phone, *"And that's why you shouldn't drink and drive, kids,"* capturing the whole aftermath of the crash like a news reporter commenting a *Public Service Announcement.*

Tony got the local dispatch on his cell phone. "Yeah hello, we need an ambulance right away at Perkins Pier – Yeah there's been a car crash and a shooting..." The dispatcher asked him some questions. "Uh no, I don't know anything about the crank call earlier, not at all. Yes, this *is* for real this time."

The rest of the night went like that for all of them; it was filled with lots of questions.

Rowan and Vang did as they'd promised and stuck to the deal they'd cut with Sheri and Jackson, implicating only Oscar in what went down. The police found Tate's Smartphone video of his murder and a few grand in cash in the burned out car that Oscar had set ablaze and figured he must have been just some crazy *Meth-head-Junky* doing another *Smash-and-Grab* job, not well planned and desperate.

They all had their pictures splashed in the

local papers for the next week.
That is until another story came along.

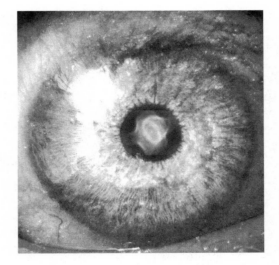

& 28 days later...
4:40 P.M.

Rowan was approaching her front door with some groceries when she stopped for a moment to look up at the sky and took a deep breath.

She marveled at the feeling that she was content with life, that the miserable past was gone and the future wide open to be shaped with joy and opportunity.

After having absorbed the epiphany, she then entered her apartment, where she found Vang was cooking dinner for the both of them.

"Hey I got the Mushrooms and the Broccoli like you asked, but they were out of Bok Choy, so I got us some Rhubarb instead."

"Thanks," he said as she put the groceries on the kitchen table.

Rowan whiffed the air; the aroma brought her to smile. "Smells wonderful," she told him, and then wandered over toward where he was standing by the stove and hugged him lovingly. "I'm so glad you could make it this weekend."

"Me too." They went to kiss each other, but before they could consummate it, there was a knock at her door.

"Hold that thought," she said to him as she answered to find a UPS deliveryman with a small package in his hands and his digital invoice pad. "Uh, Rowan Ellen?" he asked her, misreading the name.

"Ellian, and yes, that's me," she happily informed him. Not expecting any mail, she was intrigued as to what it could possibly be.

"Well sign here," he said, handing the invoice pad and the digital pen   to   her.   Rowan gleefully signed as if she were a six-year old getting a Christmas present, and when she was finished, the man handed the small box to her. "Have a nice evening," the deliveryman politely said as he left smiling at her childish response to receiving mail.

"Thanks." Rowan shut the door behind her, took the package to the kitchen table while noticing it had no return address upon it, and quickly opened it.

Inside she found a note with *a very large sum of cash*, and a *book* titled *'The Cosmos'* about the universe and the stars.

Rowan opened the letter from Sheri and Jackson, and began reading it:

Hey sugar,

My new husband and I both hope you are well. We agreed that we wanted you to have this gift - as a token of appreciation for holding up your end of the deal. You can do whatever you want with it, learn to surf, see the world, fly to the moon, whatever. But I dreamt of you using it to finally go to college and get that education you deserve. So, we can just call this the *Altruistic-Love Scholarship* if you want. Whatever you do, just do something smart with it; which I'm sure you will. Someday maybe we'll run into each other again somewhere - perhaps at your college graduation?

Love - that crazy bitch and her boyfriend:)

P.S. I knew you and Vang had the Spark of love - we're happy for you both.

Rowan was so overwhelmed with joy as she showed Vang what they had just received, pulling the wads of cash from the box, amazed and almost speechless.

Almost.

"What do you want for Dessert?" she asked with a smile ready for something sweet, as she lunged Vang with an energetic hug, and barraged him with kisses.

Rowan was ready to give him a storm of passion, in fact; *She was ready to conquer the world.*

Todd la Croix
*A.K.A **Delphius**, Is A Writer, Musician,*
Visual Artist, And Filmmaker.
If you wish to contact the Author,
You can reach him here:
delphius@live.com
http://delphius.weebly.com
http://amazon.com/author/toddlacroix

NightWave
Written by Todd La Croix
A.K.A. Delphius
The novel **NightWave** and the **Cover Art** are all

Copyright © 2011 Todd la Croix.

Dream…

28125960R00114

Made in the USA
Middletown, DE
04 January 2016